FAIREST OF ALL

A FALLEN FAIRYTALES SERIES NOVEL

A.D. ELLIS

BOOK COVERS BY SAMRAT

A.D. ELLIS

Author's Note - Content Warning

This story is darker than my usual stories. Please practice self-care and heed the content warnings below if you feel the need to do so.

Content Warnings-

This story has an MC with:

* a history of sexual abuse/trafficking (mentions of and vague descriptions of being trafficked, drugged, assaulted...no on-page rape is described)

This story also has:

* mention of an animal heart in one scene

* scenes mentioning violent revenge and revenge killing

* the MC abusing drugs in one instance early in the story

Gage ~

Bouncing around ideas for this story with you was so much fun. Thank you for...well, for just being you. You mean the world to me.

PROLOGUE

Once Upon a Time...

Nearly twenty-five years ago, his mother rested her hands on her rolling belly as her unborn son kicked and fidgeted inside on a late February afternoon. As a snowstorm blanketed the world outside her window in white, Regina DeWitt returned to the cross-stitch project she'd decided was the perfect way to while away the weeks before her baby would arrive.

When the child kicked again, Regina jerked and stabbed the soft flesh of her finger with the needle. Gasping, she grabbed her injured digit and squeezed. Drops of blood fell to the pristine white carpet of her study. Regina sucked her finger into her mouth as she studied the deep red blood on the alabaster carpet. Outside the window, an inky black bird stood in stark contrast to the blinding-white snow.

Leroy DeWitt, head of a tech company dynasty and the most powerful man in Fairwood and surrounding cities for miles and miles, entered the room, concern etched on his features. "I thought I heard you cry out. Is it the baby? Are you okay?"

Regina laughed and showed him her pricked finger. "I'm fine. This silly hobby I insisted on taking up is more painful than enjoyable. Your son is fine, strong and healthy." She gestured toward the still-wet blood shining on the white carpet and the black bird on the blanket of sparkling snow. "Many wouldn't see it as pretty, but it's all so striking. I hope our baby is just as arrestingly beautiful. White as the snow, red as the blood, and black as the bird."

Leroy studied her, love and care evident. "Our child will be as beautiful as all of that because of his stunning mother."

When their baby was born, with the palest white skin, the reddest lips, and the blackest hair, Regina's tears of joy christened him. "His name is Zane, it means snow. Zane DeWitt."

~

The DeWitts were deliriously happy for five glorious years. Zane grew into a happy, inquisitive, well-adjusted child with two parents who loved and supported him. His was the happiest of childhoods and the most powerful family in Fairwood had an amazing future ahead of them.

Until Regina DeWitt passed away suddenly, leaving Leroy and Zane devasted and alone with gaping holes where their hearts used to be.

"At least you had her for five years, my dear boy." Leroy stroked his son's black hair as the child drifted off to sleep. "Hold on to those precious memories. I know I will." The man cried himself to sleep snuggled next to Zane, thoughts of his advisers pushing him to find a new wife and provide the young DeWitt with a mother figure.

A year later, Hilary Grimstead swept into Leroy's life. He knew he would never love like he loved Regina, but his son needed a mother. Perhaps Hilary showing up in Fairwood was a sign.

Little did the poor man know what evil lurked beneath her beautiful exterior.

"Mirror, mirror, on the wall,
Who is the fairest of them all?" Hilary preened in her private quarters of the DeWitt mansion.

You are, of course, dear Hilary.

"Of course, I am. And when I marry Leroy DeWitt, I will be one step closer to taking over this whole damn town. Everyone in Fairwood will bow down to me."

. . .

With heavy persuasion from his advisers and in extreme desperation, the distraught senior DeWitt requested Hilary's hand in marriage.

"Mirror, mirror, in my hand,

Who is the fairest in the land?" The future Mrs. DeWitt smoothed her hands down her outlandishly expensive and showy purple and gold wedding dress, giddy with anticipation of their guests' shock when she walked down the aisle to marry Leroy.

You are, of course, dear Hilary.

"Of course, I am. Today, the DeWitt family empire is mine. I mustn't keep dear Leroy waiting. He's intent on marrying me and giving his brat a new mother. I do hope my beloved husband's health holds out."

Leroy DeWitt sank deeper and deeper into his despair, a shell of the man he once was. During this time, Hilary—ever the loving stepmother and perfectly doting wife in the public eye—easily talked Leroy into signing his empire over to her in the event of his death.

"Not Zane's inheritance." It was his one stipulation.

"He's lost so much, I can't stand the thought of him not being able to set out on his own when he's ready."

"He's so innocent," Hilary argued. "Do you think he'll be ready to move out at eighteen? After all he's been through?"

Leroy's eyes went distant, filling with tears. "So much for one so young."

"Make it twenty-five to give him more time to heal and adjust. If you think he's doing better at twenty, you can have it changed." Hilary shoved the pen into his hand.

Leroy nodded. "Giving him more time seems like a gift. I couldn't give him more time with his mother, but I can give him this."

Shortly after the papers were signed, Leroy fell mysteriously ill. He couldn't stand the thought of Zane suffering through his father's sickness, so the child was sent away to the best boarding school money could buy. Money was something the DeWitts had. Time, it seemed, was something Leroy DeWitt did not have.

He was dead less than a year later from an unexplainable illness.

Hilary, the grieving widow, left her stepson at the boarding school. "To save him from the darkness and grief in this house," she explained if anyone asked.

When the public eventually started making too much of a fuss regarding Zane's absence from his home and his stepmother's lack of involvement in his life, Hilary begrudgingly arranged for Zane to return to Fairwood when he was twelve.

From twelve to sixteen, Zane was mostly ignored by

Hilary. He spent most of his time with staff, went to private school, and kept to himself. He was standoffish with most people and never got close to anyone. He especially didn't trust Hilary.

His stepmother was absent the majority of the time. Zane heard whispers among the staff that she was up to no good, but he had his own grief and worries to keep him busy. She left him alone and that was a gift in and of itself.

Until she didn't.

"Mirror, mirror, gold and round,

Who is the fairest one in town?" Hilary asked on the day of Zane's sixteenth birthday.

The staff had made sure he had cake and gifts. She'd heard one of the employees teasing Zane that he'd have to start studying for his driver's license—Hilary wasn't sure about that. Giving that brat any freedom seemed like asking for troubles. She had enough balls in the air trying to juggle all of her side gigs—Hilary Grimstead-DeWitt was nothing if not resourceful, scheming, and wicked. She may have been the widow of the most powerful man in Fairwood, but that wouldn't stop her from wanting more and more and more.

And what Hilary wanted, she got. Even if it meant going out of her way, crossing lines that should never be crossed, and hurting anyone who dared to stand in her way.

Lips so red,

Raven hair upon his head,

Smooth skin white like snow,
Everyone is soon to know,
Zane DeWitt is the fairest,
His beauty is among the rarest.
Beware the child,
True and pure,
His beauty trumps yours for sure.

"What?" Hilary shrieked, launching a coffee mug toward the ornate mirror and missing by a mile as the dark liquid splattered the walls and chunks of broken glass shattered to the floor. With clenched fists, she paced and fumed. Grabbing a shard of glass, she jammed it into a photograph of Zane, the frame's glass shattering, the sharp point going straight into the child's chest. Through clenched teeth she spoke.

"Upon him, I'll cast hell and fire,
Make his beauty be for hire.
Out of my way and made to be broken,
His allure only a shiny token.
Beaten, bruised, next to nothing left,
The brat will suffer, wish for death.
End his pretty looks for good,
I shall rule over Fairwood."

As she made her plans, Hilary vowed Zane would suffer. He wouldn't ruin things for her. In fact, he'd be the perfect additional stream of income for her. She had no intention of ending him quickly and swiftly. No, he'd suffer, long and slow, learning with each passing day that he was nothing and Hilary owned him.

Only when he'd served his purpose would he be allowed to die.

And she'd make sure it was painful and slow.

No one was above her, especially not some beautiful boy named after the fucking snow.

CHAPTER 1

HOLTER TODD

I stared down at the bruised and battered body crumpled before me in the alley. *This* was the kid I'd been hired to kill and dispose of?

I'd been in Fairwood just over two months. As a child, my mother moved us from place to place, usually a new boyfriend or pimp every month. Ever since...well, ever since she'd sent me away, I'd kept up with the nomadic lifestyle.

For the first time, I questioned what I was doing with my life.

Fairwood was a somewhat strange little town. Kinda like one of those movie towns where half the town is sunshiny and perfect and half the town is gloomy and dark; everyone pretends things are happy and smiley, but there's a sinister vibe clinging to parts of the place.

I'd stopped just to spend a few days, but ended up staying longer than planned.

I'd unintentionally ended up in a great apartment with seven guys I was slowly beginning to think of as friends—something I'd never had before. It was the weirdest feeling to *want* to be around people, to look forward to seeing them, hanging out, wondering what they were up to. But the guys I'd moved in with made it easy. They almost had me thinking I didn't want to leave.

And now I studied the gorgeous, injured kid—*man*, he supposedly turned twenty-five that day—and my heart sighed. I just wasn't into it. I'd killed before. Officially, I was a bounty hunter—and now, thanks to the new crew I was living with, a bouncer at the local bar, 7—but unofficially, I was also a hitman and, generically speaking, hired muscle. People who knew the right—or wrong—people got ahold of me. If the money was right, I'd take the job.

When Hilary Grimstead-DeWitt contacted me, a few things crossed my mind. First, who was this stupid, stupid woman to contact me on her personal phone and give her real, legal name? I went through burner phones like toilet paper and hadn't given my *real* name to the people who hired me in nearly two decades.

Second, what was Grimstead-DeWitt doing hiring me at all? It took about five seconds of being in Fairwood to know she was the widow of Leroy DeWitt and the DeWitt tech dynasty was one of the most powerful in the country. The DeWitts were a powerhouse in Fairwood and for about a thousand miles in any direction. A person couldn't go anywhere in town without hearing or seeing the DeWitt name. Their mansion, their skyscraper housing hundreds of tech businesses, their home for children looking for a forever family, the main street going through the heart of downtown, hell, even a lot of businesses in town boasted the DeWitt name. Rumor had it that the late Leroy DeWitt had been a kind, generous, and socially-conscious businessman along with his first wife, while his new wife was...well, *not* any of those things.

Hilary Grimstead-DeWitt seemed to personify that aforementioned sinister vibe. So, again, while it was in keeping with what I'd heard about her, what in the ever-loving-fuck was Hilary doing hiring me to kill her stepson? She was either the dumbest, most naïve woman in the world, or she was so confident in her name and place that she thought herself above getting caught.

Did it matter?

I'd killed before. That wasn't the problem.

True, the first time I'd killed someone was protecting someone I loved. Fuckin' lot of good that did me.

However, murder-for-hire was something I took very seriously, and I'd only killed when the mark was a menace to society—the worst of the worst.

I got no thrill from killing and wouldn't invite karma to kick my ass by taking out someone who didn't deserve to be offed.

Looks could be deceiving, but the guy on the ground in front of me didn't look the least bit like a monster deserving to be murdered.

Hilary had agreed to my stipulation of finding Zane DeWitt *first* and then I'd decide if I'd take the job. Again, either dumb or dangerously confident. Or even worse, a psychopath.

The man on the ground had the palest skin I'd ever seen. Even mottled black and blue with bruises, the untouched parts were like alabaster. His inky black hair contrasted starkly with his pale skin, the bleeding wound matting his dark locks into thick, wet clumps.

And his lips.

Fuck.

His lips.

Were they blood red from his injuries? Had to be, right? No one's lips were *that* red. Full, plump, the perfect little cupid's bow.

I couldn't kill this man.

At least not while he lay suffering in a battered, bruised, and broken heap.

Glancing around the alley to be sure no one was watching, I knelt and gently touched his shoulder. The head wound bled like a stuck hog, but head wounds did that. I was more concerned about a concussion. Broken ribs, bruised spleen, punctured lungs.

He moaned, the pained sound filling the air and bouncing off the alley walls.

Fighting through the pain and swelling, he cracked one eye. Through the bruising, I lost myself in the deepest, darkest brown.

Even in his current state, he was absolutely gorgeous.

No. I couldn't kill this man.

Something told me Zane DeWitt was going to change my life.

For better or worse? That remained to be seen.

But for the time being, my protective instincts kicked in and I was determined to help this kid.

Did it have anything to do with the unexplainable, long-buried emotions he stirred in me?

Maybe. But now wasn't the time to delve into *that* analysis.

Did I have a single clue why his broken body, deep brown eyes, and striking beauty gave me pause in a way I'd never experienced before?

No.

But I knew I wasn't offing him. Not now.

I just needed a way to keep Hilary off his tail and help him heal.

Checking my watch, I calculated I had a few hours before Hilary would expect a call from me to let her know if I was accepting the hit or not.

That gave me plenty of time.

"Hey, princess, you with me?" I brushed the ebony hair from his forehead.

Zane moaned and said something I couldn't hear.

I leaned in closer. "Say it again."

"Fuck. You."

The words were strained, but they brought a smile to my face.

Zane DeWitt was a fighter.

"That's it, princess, stay feisty."

This was going to be fun.

CHAPTER 2
ZANE DEWITT

I drifted in and out of consciousness, pain coursing through me with each beat of my heart.

But my heart continued beating and that was what mattered.

Every throbbing, white-hot shot of pain screaming through me reminded me I was alive.

And for the time being, I'd take it.

I hadn't been surprised when my stepmother's goons surrounded me as I left my father's mansion to visit the bank and take care of getting my inheritance transferred to my account.

Hilary Grimstead married my father for one reason and one reason only.

The DeWitt name.

With that name came money.

And power.

My late parents had used their name for good.

Hilary didn't have a good bone in her body.

The pain and trauma I'd been subjected to since my

father died was proof of that. When my stepmother pulled me from my peaceful grieving at boarding school, I found myself back home and more distraught than ever without my father. But I'd been left alone, ignored by Hilary, cared for by staff, and content in my studies at a prestigious private school.

All of that changed at sixteen. It was like a switch had flipped and Hilary became determined to break me. At that point in time, and for the next nine years, the abuse she allowed me to endure—forced me to endure, sold me into, took absolute pleasure in watching—seemed to be for two main reasons. One, break me until I ended myself or perished in the process. Two, the massive amounts of money rich people were willing to pay for my body.

Hilary made no secret that the DeWitt name, power, and money were everything she'd ever hoped for. But she also made it clear she'd never stop wanting more. More power, more money, more lives she could crush in her cold, dead hands.

As memories of what I'd survived for all those years came rushing back, I welcomed the searing pain in my chest and the excruciating throbbing in my head as my current injuries took me away from the blazing-hot pain of the past.

Twenty-five.

I'd only had to make it to twenty-five.

Then my inheritance was mine and I could leave.

Turn her in, see her pay for all she'd done to me.

Could I have left all those years ago?

Of course.

But the first time I tried to escape, Hilary made sure I

knew my leaving wouldn't stop the abuse. The money paid for my body would continue to come in. She'd just provide other subjects for the buyers.

When I'd looked confused, wondering where she'd get others to sell to the highest bidders, she'd thrown her head back and cackled. "Have you visited the DeWitt Children's Home lately, Zaney? All of those beautiful children wishing desperately for a forever home. Imagine their joy turned to terror when they pack their belongings and move in with their new family only to find out they've left bad for worse. You'd be throwing them straight from the pot right into the fire." She'd watched me shrewdly. "Yes, I can see it in your eyes. As badly as you want to escape the pain, you'd never subject those children to your fate. And what a terrible thing to have your father's good name sullied—it wouldn't take much to spread rumors around town that Leroy started that home so he'd have children at his beck and call." A blood-red fingernail trailed down my cheek. "As long as you keep our buyers happy with your perfect little body, I won't ever have to resort to shopping for new meat at the home or convincing people Leroy DeWitt was a pedophile."

That day, my fate had been sealed. I'd shut everything out, taken the abuse, and focused on turning twenty-five. Back then, it had seemed like a lifetime away, but knowing I was saving the children from the nightmare I lived made it somewhat easier to deal with. And I'd protect my father's name with everything I had. I wanted to think no one who knew him would ever believe Hilary's lies about him, but he'd been gone for so long and...I just didn't know anymore.

So, I'd bided my time. Kept track of names, faces, dates, and acts inflicted upon me. Fairwood would soon know the real Hilary Grimstead. The city would learn the dark, dirty secrets so many of their top residents kept hidden. CEOs, financial advisers, presidents of companies, high-ranking political figures, successful entrepreneurs, philanthropists, housewives—there wasn't a single sector of the city's upper echelon I didn't have dirt on.

And I'd spill each and every name.

Happily, and with malice.

I'd watch them all go down in flames for each and every heinous act they forced on me. I'd watch them all burn.

But none would bring as much satisfaction as watching Hilary Grimstead lose everything. The DeWitt name. The power. The money.

She'd be left with nothing.

And then?

Well, then I'd kill her.

Hilary's men had beaten me to a pulp and left me in an alleyway. I knew I needed to get up and disappear before too long, but the pain overshadowed everything. They'd be back. Or Hilary would send someone else. Now that I was old enough to get the money and get away, she'd be desperate to see me gone.

Before I'd turned twenty-five, Hilary held all the cards. She lorded the children over me. She controlled pretty much every job in town one way or another. Even if I'd been able to land a job, any application for buying a car, renting an apartment, hell, just trying to get a credit card, all of those things would somehow be known to her. I had no way to leave Fairwood, even if I wanted to run away from the only home I'd ever known—the home my father built for me.

I'd watched for over a decade as Hilary broke people, ruined their lives. And it never seemed to be for any reason other than she wanted to or she perceived they'd wronged her some way. I never knew *how* she controlled so much in Fairwood and beyond, but she did. Based on the way she'd controlled me for so long, I assumed she had most of the others in the same sort of powerless situation.

Now that I was twenty-five—the age she'd convinced my father I needed to be to inherit the money he wanted me to have—she no longer had the law on her side in regards to the money my father left me. With anyone else, that would have maybe been a good thing. With Hilary, it just meant she'd get more desperate and stoop even lower to make sure I was out of the picture.

Was it because she knew what all I had on her? Yeah, I was sure that was part of it. But there was something so deeply disturbed and sinister about her—some obsessive reason she hated me so much and wanted me out of her life. Hilary was so fucked up, she was likely less concerned with me turning her in to the authorities and more fixated on seeing me dead if I was no longer going to be available for her and others to torment and traumatize. Money and power meant more to her than the possible punishment for what she'd done—honestly, I didn't think she even cared about the consequences… almost as if she didn't think the law could touch her.

As I drifted in and out of the hazy pain, I became aware of someone else in the alley. Big, black boots. Someone tall. Based on the foot size, I guessed a male someone. Fear washed over me. Was this who Hilary had sent to finish the job? Or was this just some rando in the alleyway looking to use me? Some people got off on bringing pain to someone already in great pain.

Ask me how I knew.

When his knees popped and he knelt next to me, I wished like hell I was able to roll away and run. But the pain immobilized me and I had no choice; I was stuck.

"Hey, princess, you with me?" He brushed a wet chunk of hair from my forehead.

I moaned and did my best to form words through my busted-up lips.

The big man leaned in closer. "Say it again."

"Fuck. You." My words were strained, but I wasn't going down without a fight.

"That's it, princess, stay feisty."

My gut twisted.

This wasn't going to be fun.

CHAPTER 3
HOLTER

I'd been looking for Zane on foot that day, so I called a ride. Kinda like an Uber or Lyft, but more on the underbelly of the city's riff-raff. When you'd been roaming and crossing the lines of morality as long as I had, you found the darker side of a place real quick. My connections had connections no matter which city I ended up in. I often needed a ride; one that wouldn't ask questions and would conveniently not remember anything about the 6'3", two-hundred-thirty-pound inked man they picked up and dropped off. My motorcycle was useful for traveling, but I did most of my in-city work on foot.

"Come on," I said as I hefted Zane's slim body into my arms. "Let's get you cleaned up and some rest."

Like a cat in a bathtub, Zane clawed and scratched like his life depended on it.

"Hey," I grumbled as I tried to place him as gently as possible into the back seat of the dark sedan. "I'm not trying to hurt you. Stop." I mean, if I'd taken Hilary's job,

I would have been trying to *kill* him, but he didn't know that.

Zane continued to fight me, mumbling something about "they all want to hurt me" before succumbing to the pain of his injuries and curling in on himself as the car's rolling motion subdued him.

What the hell had happened to him? Why was he beaten and left in an alley on his twenty-fifth birthday? And why did one of the most powerful women in Fairwood want her stepson dead?

While the car drove to the address I'd given, I reached out to a few people in search of an item I needed if I was going to get Hilary off Zane's back. The third text I sent yielded what I was looking for. We arranged for a delivery and payment. Once I contacted Hilary and provided her the proof I'd taken care of Zane, I'd destroy my current phone and grab a new one.

My next call was to one of my roommates, Asa. He was a doctor at the local clinic and I had no doubt he'd be able to help get Zane patched up. Asa was brilliant and could have been a surgeon at the Fairwood Hospital—one of the top hospitals in the nation—but his heart was in providing care to those who needed it most.

"Hello?" Asa said as he picked up.

For their part, my roommates had been pretty accommodating when it came to my burner phones, weird hours, and morally gray situations I couldn't really tell them about. "It's Holter," I said, knowing Asa wouldn't recognize the number I was calling from.

"Holt." I heard the soft smile in Asa's voice. "What's up? Can you do dinner with us tonight?"

Something weird tugged in my chest, but I pushed it aside. "Um, yeah, probably. Listen, I've got a situation that needs your help. What time will you be home?" Calling a place *home* was a completely foreign concept for me, but I forged on.

"My shift is over soon. Why, what's going on?"

"I'll be home in a bit." I glanced at Zane. "Can you bring some first-aid supplies? Maybe some pain medication?"

"Holt, I—" he started.

"Just the supplies. I'll get the pain meds." I had no trouble crossing lines myself, and putting people in bad situations in the past had never been a concern, but I just couldn't do it with my new roommates. They'd been so great—a lot better to me than I deserved—and I wouldn't ask Asa to break any rules and risk his job.

Not for me.

And not for...

Zane moaned.

Something told me I'd demand the world break every rule known if it meant protecting this beautiful man. And what the fuck was that? I was a protector in my own right, but I didn't get protective over specific people. I took care of myself and helped get rid of humanity's worst. I fucked around; I didn't catch feelings.

Shut the fuck up. These aren't feelings. You're confused about the hit. Worried about his injuries. Planning how to cover things up and throw Hilary off. Period. End of story.

I didn't let myself think one second longer about why my heart squeezed possessively with each pump of blood through my veins. Didn't acknowledge the weird rush of *whatever* that was in my chest from the moment I saw Zane on the ground. I wasn't a hero. I wasn't looking to settle down. And I damn sure wasn't one to allow my heart to get involved with anything.

Fuck. As far as I was concerned, I didn't *have* a heart. I'd get Zane patched up, make sure he was safe, and be on my merry way. That was life for me. I didn't stay in one place too long.

True, I'd never opted for a place with a nine-month lease. The hits and bounties in my past had been kept as anonymous as possible. I was in and out, quick and efficient. I tracked down and brought in the bad guys. Or I found them and took them out. Usually for the safety of others, sometimes just because the scum had pissed me off by resembling my past.

Finding myself thinking about Zane's health and safety was new.

And I didn't like it.

Except when he whimpered as we hit a nasty pothole and I wondered...hell, I wondered *everything* about him. And that was a fucking trip. I didn't wonder about people. I didn't concern myself with the human side of things.

Until, it seemed, I found a bloody Zane DeWitt and my fucking heart decided to short circuit.

I should drop him at the Fairwood Hospital. Just drop him and go. Pack up my belongings and head out. I could be to a new city within hours. Find a seedy hotel, rest for a few days, and put this whole damn place out of my head. Forget the men I stupidly started thinking of as possible, actual friends. Clear my mind of the beautiful, broken boy someone wanted dead.

That's what I should have done.

Instead...

Instead, I brushed a lock of black, black hair from his forehead and wiped a trickle of blood from his temple.

And wondered what he looked like when he smiled.

The car hit a few more potholes. We were definitely heading into the sketchier part of town. I always picked the shady part of a new place. I blended in better there. I was a big guy, a few visible scars—a lifetime of emotional ones—several tattoos, dressed in black, riding a motorcycle. The more unsavory a part of town, the more likely I was not to be noticed.

When the car pulled up to The Woods, I handed the driver some cash. He was seasoned, accustomed to sneaking around and keeping things quiet; I could see it in his eyes. The man nodded and I got out of the car. Going to the other side, I got Zane out as carefully as I could—ignoring the tiny grunts of pain coming from his pretty red lips—and made my way to the door.

The Woods was in a bad part of town and it totally looked the part. When I'd first arrived in Fairwood, I'd planned to grab a rent-by-the-week hotel room, but I'd seen a sign for a room for rent when I'd stopped for a to-go cup of black sludge at the shitty gas station on the corner. The picture of The Woods had looked so bad, I couldn't help but check it out.

And it was bad.

So bad.

From the outside, it looked as if it were about to be

condemned. It needed new paint, new shingles, new gutters, new *everything*, but walking through the door to The Woods blanketed me in something I couldn't even explain. And when I saw the actual apartment and rooms, I realized it was the epitome of a diamond in the rough.

I'd met Asa that day. He'd shown me around the place and told me he and some of his friends owned it. Asa explained they let the outside look like shit so it didn't call attention to them. There were seven people living there and they all slept better knowing no one would target The Woods when it looked like it was one second away from mandated demolition.

"We keep it just this side of meeting city codes on the outside," Asa had told me. "But the inside is our own little fairytale."

The building was an old dormitory that had once housed families of patients at a nearby hospital. This was before the old hospital had been torn down and the new one built in the better part of town. But several years ago, if a patient was confined to the hospital for a long stay due to severe illness or long-term treatment, the hospital would offer the family a room at The Woods.

The one-story building had been left vacant when the old hospital closed down, but someone bought it before it met the same demolition fate as the hospital. The buyer had transformed the inside, but the renovation had stopped before they'd gotten to the outside. Asa and his friends bought the place for cheap and moved in a couple years ago.

As I carried Zane inside, I thought about the seven

men I lived with. They were friends from childhood, more like a family. They were all very different, but the thread of friends-as-family was evident in everything they did.

Asa was the doctor. Gorgeous, caring, and so damn smart.

Dodie split his time as a bouncer or filling in behind the bar at 7. He was the one who suggested I grab some hours as a bouncer there as well. His real name was Dwayne Dodieu, but everyone called him Dodie. The name fit the goofy, caring man much better.

I'd quickly learned that Doc and Dodie had a thing for each other. I read people very easily. Asa basically fell all over himself whenever Dodie was around. Dodie felt the same for Asa, but believed he was too dumb and dopey for a guy as smart as the doc.

My new bosses at 7 were happy-go-lucky Felix and his complete opposite, Aiden. Felix was the sunshine to Aiden's grumpiness and they ran 7 like a well-oiled machine. The two really shouldn't have worked together, but they somehow made it look easy.

Lorien was a massage therapist and acupuncturist specializing in insomnia and other sleep-related issues. From the bits and pieces I'd gleaned in my time there, I'd figured out Lorien was asexual. He was perfectly content with his found family, but he wouldn't be partnering up with any of them outside of being close, lifetime friends.

Concord and Swayze rounded out the group of seven. Concord was a straight-laced, bashful therapist. As much as I did my best to avoid being psychoanalyzed, I felt completely at ease with the guy. If I ever found myself not living with him, he was probably the only person I'd ever consider spilling my guts to.

Swayze was a landscaper. The guy probably had the worst outdoor allergies I'd ever seen in a person. Made his job all the more difficult, but he loved being outside and had a real talent for creating artwork with grass, plants, trees, and mulch. And he kept the allergy medicine companies in business pretty much all year round.

Pausing briefly, unsure of when I'd started thinking of this place as *home*, I thought of the rooms and pairings. The building was a square with nine rooms on the outside with a kitchen and living room in the middle. Each room had its own tiny bathroom, a closet, a window, and space for a bed, dresser, and desk or recliner. The entryway led from the front door right into the living room and was made up of a little hallway and half-bath.

The room to the immediate right of the entry hall was a single occupied by Lorien.

The next two rooms were connected and shared by Aiden and Felix. They'd set theirs up to be one bedroom and one living area of sorts.

The next room was empty and connected to my room by a shared inner door. When I'd moved in, they'd let me pick which room I wanted. I'd put zero thought into it because I didn't think I'd be there long. Now though, I found the space comforting, almost like a sanctuary to escape to when the demons in my head got too loud.

Concord and Swayze resided in the next two rooms, also connected by a door. On the brief tour I'd been given, it appeared they'd kept their rooms separate, but I knew they switched beds every other night or so because they joked about needing to clean the sheets.

The final two connecting rooms were occupied by Asa and Dodie. I imagined the two of them pining away for each other from their separate beds every night. I'd never been a romantic—love wasn't something I had much experience with—but watching the two of them together gave me some sort of weird, schmoozy, hopeful feeling. If anyone was going to find their forever—or whatever shit people wanted to say about love—I hoped it was Doc and Dodie.

As I held Zane in my arms, I thought through where I should put him. The couch, in my bed, or in the unoccupied room were options. The couch wasn't all that comfortable and he wouldn't have any privacy. It might freak him out to wake up in a stranger's bed—plus, he might take a bit to recover and I wasn't getting into co-sleeping.

He got the empty room.

The bed was made up with a simple cheap, white sheet. Zane's injuries would make a mess of it, but I'd get him something nicer.

Nicer than what a DeWitt is used to? Dream on.

Placing him gently on the bed, I grabbed the light blanket hanging over the footboard and spread it out over his broken body.

Where was Asa?

I shot a text to my contact from earlier and added in payment for pain medication. Then I texted Lorien and asked if he'd be able to get nice sheets, a blanket, and something to help a person relax and feel comfortable.

Lorien: Sure. What's up?

Me: Just need to make sure someone can rest and relax. I'll explain more when you're home.

Lorien: :) okay, I'll pick some things up on the way.

Me: Thank you.

The front door opened as I tried to reconcile this whole having friends, leaning on others, and the warmth spreading through my chest.

Glancing at Zane to make sure he was breathing, I walked out of his room to meet Asa.

"Before you say anything, I'll cover his part of the rent until he's healed up and can decide if he wants to stay or not." The words were out of my mouth before my brain had time to contemplate exactly what I was saying. The rent wasn't a problem—it was actually dirt-cheap and money wasn't something I was short on...my line of work brought in plenty of revenue—but what was I doing offering up a room to Zane DeWitt?

Asa cocked a brow. "I feel like maybe I need to catch up. Who is *he*? What happened?"

I threw a look over my shoulder. "Can I wait to tell

the story once everyone is here?" The guys weren't used to me telling lots of details, but it would be easier to explain to everyone just once. I couldn't ask them to bring Zane into their home without making sure they knew what was going on.

Asa studied me, likely wondering what was so different with this situation that I'd be willing to give even a few details. It was fair of him to wonder—I was doing much the same.

"Of course. Let everyone know we need to have a house meeting this evening before Aiden and Felix head to work. I think Dodie has a shift tonight..." Asa paused, his cheeks pinking. "But we can all meet before they leave."

I nodded and looked again at the spare room.

Asa held up a little medical supply bag. "Take me to my patient."

CHAPTER 4
ZANE

The voices I heard murmuring outside the door didn't sound threatening. I'd been in enough really bad situations to pick up on when something was about to get ugly; my gut wasn't sending up warning signs this time. So, instead of my fight or flight instinct kicking in or my head taking me deep into shut-down mode, I just let my body rest.

Every so often, I cracked a swollen eye and took in the room around me. It was sparsely furnished with cheap sheets on the bed, a built-in closet, a bedside table, and a desk with a chipped corner. Nothing like the lavish furnishings I'd grown up with, but this place felt safer than my "home" had felt in several years.

The sheets weren't super soft, but the bed was better than the asphalt I'd been curled up on an hour or so ago. The men outside my room were talking in easy tones, they weren't here to hurt me. My body ached, but I knew from past experiences that my injuries weren't as severe as ones I'd dealt with before.

All-in-all, I was alive and I was going to be okay despite a few days of painful healing—stiff muscles, ugly bruises, and the mind-fuck my head would inevitably send me into.

With the men still talking in low voices just outside my room, I switched my thoughts to the money. Hilary couldn't touch my inheritance, but I didn't put it past her to fuck something up with it. I needed to get to the bank and get it all worked out—probably needed to get in contact with my father's attorney as well. The sooner I had that money in my possession, the sooner I could move on, heal, and destroy Hilary Grimstead.

The biggest concern nagging me at that moment was what Hilary's plan had been with her men beating me up. Was it just to stop me from getting to the bank? If that was the case, she should have known me well enough to know a beat-down wasn't going to hold me up for long.

Were the men supposed to do worse than rough me up and leave me? There was no way they thought I was dead when they dropped me in that alley. So, what went wrong? Was someone else supposed to come and finish the job?

The door cracked open and I tensed on instinct. Nothing about this place made me afraid, but years of conditioning had my body and mind going into survival mode when someone walked into my room. Through heavy lashes and swollen eyes, I took in the man who'd brought me here moving to the desk and leaning against it, his arms crossed menacingly, but his eyes watching me with concern.

The man who approached the bed carried a bag of sorts. He spoke softly, "Hi, Zane. My name is Asa. I'm a doctor. Holter brought you here because he was worried about your injuries. Would you be okay with me taking a look and trying to fix you up?"

I let my eyes flutter open. "I'm fine."

The man at the desk, Holter, scoffed. "Whatever you say, princess."

Asa shot him a look while continuing to speak to me. "Do you know if you lost consciousness? We're worried about internal injuries, a concussion...I'd like to get you cleaned up and make sure you're not in need of anything more than the basics."

Based on the light outside and the time I'd been heading to the bank, I knew I hadn't lost any huge chunks of time. "Didn't lose consciousness. I've had internal bleeding before—this isn't it. Bruised ribs, not broken. Head hurts, but not bad enough to have a concussion. They roughed me up, but they weren't trying to kill me."

Holter shifted and something crossed his face. "Let him fix you up and get you some pain meds—we need to talk."

"About what?" I challenged.

Holter's jaw clenched. "Trust me."

I snorted, my chest only slightly aching. "I've spent way too long being made to do things I most definitely didn't want to do by people I sure as shit didn't trust, so excuse me all to hell if I don't trust someone I just met."

The argument was valid, but the weird thing was that I trusted Holter and Asa. I wasn't sure why, didn't know what it meant, but my gut told me I was safe with them.

Holter's nostrils flared. "Fair enough. Can Asa please patch you up, get you some medication, and then we can talk about Hilary Grimstead."

My stomach clenched. Holter knew Hilary. Maybe I'd read the situation wrong. I studied the big man before glancing at Asa. No, these men didn't want to hurt me. But what did Holter know about Hilary?

I breathed as deep as bruised ribs would allow and rolled to my back, shifting up into a slightly reclined position against the pillow.

"I have a hospital gown if you'd like some privacy to put it on?" Asa reached for a light blue cloth inside the opening of his bag.

Catching Holter's eyes, I shook my head. In the past, I didn't get a choice. Now, I was in control. I had no doubt he'd argue it, but Holter would leave with Asa if I asked them to. They'd respect my wishes if I said no to an exam or if I asked for privacy to change.

That knowledge left me with a powerful, floaty feeling—an energy, a challenge, something spurring me on.

"I don't need a gown." Gently lifting my shirt over my head, I held back any gasps of pain trying to escape. The material was covered in blood, but it was the only clothing I had for the time being. So, I rolled it as neatly as possible and placed it to the side. Maybe they'd let me borrow the washing machine before I left.

Shimmying out of my pants, wondering briefly if Holter would have opinions on my rainbow bikinis, I winced as the elastic rubbed against the sensitive pink scars on my hips and the road rash on my outer thighs.

In only my underwear and socks, the room suddenly took on a chill.

Holter immediately messed with the thermostat and I couldn't help but be grateful for that simple gesture.

"I'd like to check your injuries from bottom to top," Asa said, touching a gentle hand to my foot. He worked my feet over, palpating and asking questions before working his way up my legs. "Mostly bumps and bruises, but I recognize several old injuries."

"Yeah, you do."

"These aren't new," Asa said, not asking a question when his gloved fingers grazed over the raised pink scars I kept hidden on my hips.

"Nope."

"Let's get them washed and covered. Infection is a risk with cuts like these, but they mostly appear to be healed." Asa prepped a cloth with antiseptic. "This shouldn't hurt since the wounds aren't open."

"Can't hurt any worse than putting them there." The first few times I cut myself, I felt guilty and ashamed even though the pain I inflicted on my own flesh helped to block out the torturous pain the people who bought my body caused. From sixteen to nineteen, I fought hard against those who purchased me. As the years went on, I cycled through cutting and healing—harming myself to have something to focus on rather than the physical and psychological pain of what the buyers did to me.

And my own traitorous body.

I hadn't cut for a very long time, but the old scars—

some of which hadn't healed well—were always there as a reminder.

Reminders of what I'd endured.

Reminders of the children I'd protected.

Reminders of the revenge I'd get against those who hurt me.

Reminders of why I wanted Hilary Grimstead dead.

At nineteen, I'd made the decision to bear the abuse to save the children...to tolerate what they put my body and mind through...not to fight it even when it curled my stomach and sent me into a nightmare world of pain and suffering...that was when I took back a bit of power and stopped cutting.

For the most part.

I told Hilary I wouldn't try to run; I'd be her pawn and money-maker until I was twenty-five. Once she knew I wasn't going to leave, she agreed to letting me have a bit of freedom. As long as I was available for what she called *appointments* and as long as I played the part the buyer wanted, I wasn't relegated to my room and locked away like I had been from sixteen to nineteen.

I finished my courses and earned two degrees—all online as I had to be readily available for appointments. Predators didn't follow a school-day schedule.

The buyers paid for my body and they still hurt me, but choosing to approach it as a business transaction—a really shitty one where I got used and hurt and only Hilary got the proceeds—allowed me to compartmentalize the pain and led me to stop cutting.

Mostly.

I still had moments where it got to be too much and I'd seek out the release self-harm brought.

"What the fuck did she do to you?" Holter growled as he pushed off from the desk and paced the room.

"There's not enough time left this year to start that story." My words, laced with angry bitterness, brought the big man to a halt.

His teeth gritted together and hate filled his face. He was definitely someone I wanted on my side and not fighting against me.

"I may be able to get something to lessen the scarring," Asa said as he finished cleaning the area. "Can I examine your belly and torso? I want to listen to your heart and lungs."

"Go for it."

The doc set to work on my belly and my ribs, asking me for deep breaths and listening closely with his stethoscope. When he moved to my head, I winced. "You may need stitches on this gash."

"You check it out, but I'd really rather just wash up real good and see if maybe some butterflies might do the job."

"Stubborn little shit," Holter grumbled.

"My body, my head wound," I shot back. "I'm never going back to what that bitch put me through. I control what I do with my body every second of the day from now on." My chest burned with each painful breath, but I meant every word I said.

I had dreams of falling in love, of sharing earth-shattering intimacy with the man I chose to share my life and my body with. Even taking the steps to remove myself from Hilary's evil and take back control of my body and my choices, I feared none of that would ever happen.

But I wouldn't ever let someone else make decisions about my body again.

Holter moved closer to the bed and cupped my chin. "Get one thing straight, I will *never* take away your choices or your control over your own body. But maybe you can stop being a damn stubborn little princess and let the doctor fix you up so you can heal right and not end up with permanent damage."

Swallowing thickly, lost in Holter's dark eyes, I nodded. "If I need stitches, that's fine. I trust you." The words were meant for Asa, but the trust applied to both men, and that was an absolutely foreign feeling.

An hour later, I was showered and wearing someone else's pajamas. Under the bright light of the bathroom, Asa dried and cleaned the gash on my head, numbed the area, and stitched me up while Holter and a man named Lorien stripped the bed I'd been in and made it up with new sheets and a blanket.

When Asa guided me back toward the bed, a yawn cracked my jaw.

"Here, I got some medication for you. You can sleep for a little bit. We'll talk with all the guys later." Holter held out a bottle for me.

"I'm not taking drugs."

"It's not drugs," Holter started. "I mean, it's pain medication, but it's legal."

"No, thanks."

"It will help you sleep."

"I don't take anything from anyone I don't know. Been there, done that, have the physical and psychological scars to prove it." Nightmare-ish images barged through my head. Needles shoved into my flesh to inject me with chemicals. Pills crushed and forced down my throat. Men and women encouraging me to drink with them so I'd loosen up quicker thanks to whatever cocktail they'd laced the alcohol with.

In a way, I should have been grateful for the drugs because they often took me so far out of the situation that I barely recalled anything more than the worst pain and the most terrible images.

But they also made it so I had absolutely no control over what went on. Not that I could have stopped it. The worst was the vasodilators mixed with any other chemical—I'd be out of it, but my body would respond as if I wanted what was being done to me. It was the most helpless feeling in the world to be assaulted and crying out in pain even as my body appeared to be enjoying what was happening. I think a lot of the buyers used my erections and orgasms to comfort themselves into thinking they weren't hurting me too badly if I was hard and got off. But most of them requested Hilary give me the Viagra-like drugs, so it wasn't like they thought I was getting hard on my own.

In my worst recurring nightmares, the memories of the pain woke me, but the most haunting part was how badly I begged my body not to respond only to have my attackers touch me and comment about what a good boy I was, getting so hard for them. How I was such a hungry little slut for them, look how much I wanted it. Look how hard I came.

"It's not to hurt you," Holter argued.

"I'll take ibuprofen if I can see it's in a sealed container from Asa."

Holter's jaw clenched again, but Asa placed a hand on the bigger man's forearm.

"I've got sealed packets of extra-strength ibuprofen," the doc said. "Will that work?"

I nodded. "Thanks."

"I'm not trying to hurt you," Holter growled.

"Everyone in my life since my dad died has wanted to hurt me. It's not you, it's me; I don't trust people."

A shadow of something crossed Holter's face and feelings I wasn't used to washed through me.

Swallowing thickly, I said, "If it makes you feel any better, I feel safer here with you and the doc than any time in my life since I was sixteen. So, deep down, I must know you're not trying to hurt me. I just have a lot of shit to work through."

Holter looked like he wanted to ask something, say something, but he didn't. He just nodded. "Take what Asa can give you. I'll let you sleep for a bit. We need to talk with all the guys before Felix, Aiden, and Dodie head to work tonight."

I hadn't left the little room I was in and my eyes shot to the door. "Damn, how many people live here?" A frisson of fear shot through me as memories of the four men who once bought me at a premium price attacked my mind.

"There are seven guys, plus me." Holter held up a

hand at what must have been panic on my face. “It’s okay. I have just as many trust issues as you do. I’ve never once felt concern about any of these men. They are good and safe. I don’t really have friends, but they’re as close as I’d consider to being my friends.” He scowled. “If I was looking for friends.”

The day was catching up with me and I yawned again as Asa returned with water and a packet of ibuprofen. “These should help take the edge off. If you want something stronger, I can get it.”

I shook my head and swallowed the pills. “I’m good. If I was in more pain, I’d maybe take something since it would be my choice, but I’m really not hurting that badly.” At least not physically. Emotionally, I was fucked up. Mentally, my head was trying to wrap around how to protect the children’s home, ruin every person who had ever hurt me, and kill Hilary.

“I’ll wake you up in a couple hours.” Holter locked my door and then headed for the second door in the back corner. “This connects to my room. I’m locking it too. You’re safe in here, you have my word. Sleep.”

For the first time since Hilary sold my body to the highest bidder, I actually felt safe enough to let down my guard and sleep. Hilary wasn’t going to just give up on me and I had to be ever-aware, watchful, prepared, but I may have just found my first ever soft landing place since my dad died.

CHAPTER 5
HOLTER

"He's been through a lot," Asa said softly, his hand on my shoulder. "Be patient with him. I only saw the physical, I'm sure the psychological is a thousand times worse."

I gritted my teeth. "If someone was hurting him, why'd he stay?" It was a stupid question. I'd seen my own mom suffer for years. Guy after guy roughing her up. She never left until *he* moved on or kicked her to the curb in favor of fresh meat. I knew there were five thousand reasons for people not leaving bad situations.

I'd lived it.

"That's for Zane to say." Asa organized his medical bag and put it near the door. "But people in bad situations often have several reasons they don't leave. It's easy for those of us on the outside to think they should have just walked out, but the person living the situation sees it in a very different light."

"Why the scars on his hips? Why cut yourself if you're already being hurt in other ways?"

"Some of us turn to alcohol or drugs to numb the pain. Some use sex or gambling. Some spend money." Asa shrugged. "Some people self-harm. The pain of the cutting or burning or whatever method they use helps to dull the other pain. In most situations, the person being harmed has no control over the situation, so they use the self-harm as something they can control. It's trading one bad thing for another, but at least they control it and the pain they give themselves blocks out the other, for a little while."

My stomach roiled. What in the hell had Zane lived through that meant taking a razor blade to his own perfect porcelain skin was an answer? And what had made him stay? My mind was going a million miles a minute trying to block out all the heinous acts he may have endured—I wanted to be wrong, but I had a feeling I was maybe not even close to how bad it really was.

"Let's give him a couple hours to sleep," Asa said.

I glanced at my phone. "Yeah, I have some work to do. Did you let the guys know we need to talk?"

He nodded. "They'll all be here. Maybe you fill us all in a bit first, then we wake Zane and let him meet everyone?"

"I can do that."

Asa touched my shoulder again. "He's welcome here for as long as needed. We can discuss rent at another time."

"Thanks." I looked at the closed door where Zane slept. "I don't know his story. Part of me doesn't want to know his story. But the other part of me thinks I'm already in too deep and I need to let it play out."

Asa smiled softly. “Sometimes life doesn’t go the way we expect it to. It’s not always a bad thing to have something unexpected stop us in our tracks.”

I took his words with me as I went outside to make a few phone calls.

In the end, I had the two things I needed. They’d cost me a pretty penny, but they’d hopefully buy Zane a bit of safety and freedom.

I called Hilary.

“’Bout time you called,” she snapped.

“Who do you think this is?” I asked.

She paused and I imagined her shrewd eyes narrowing. “I assume it’s the man I...well, the man I hired to do a service for me.”

“The man you hired to *kill* your stepson? Who now has your real name and your phone number?” I asked.

“Only thugs and common criminals use burner phones.”

“Only fools use their own phone to plan murder for hire schemes.”

“I don’t have time for this. Did you find him? Is it done?”

The woman was a piece of work.

“I found him. It’s done.”

“How do I know you’re telling the truth?”

“I guess you don’t. I’ve got photos if you want them.”

“Send them to my email. I’ll text it to you. Once I see the proof, I’ll send the money.”

“You’ll send half the money now. Then I’ll give you the proof. Hang up. I’ll send you the wire transfer information.” She started to argue, but I ended the call.

Once I sent her the untraceable link to wire the payment to me, I waited.

The area outside of The Woods wasn't the best. Not bright and welcoming, not a place to sit and relax while taking in the sun and fresh air. We were too far away from the elite of the city for that. But the bench I sat on next to a run-down playground put me right in the warm rays of sunshine as a soft late-fall breeze blew. It had been years since I'd allowed myself to slow down long enough to notice the breeze. Years since I'd let down my guard enough to recognize the hidden beauty in a place.

Why now? What was it about Fairwood that called to me? Had me staying put for the first time in years? I glanced at The Woods and pictured Zane sleeping. Broken and beautiful. He appeared delicate—almost fragile—but I sensed a strength to him the likes of which many would never understand.

My gut churned. I wanted to protect him. Like a rope tethered to him from deep inside my soul, something pulled me to Zane DeWitt. I didn't like it. Getting involved spelled trouble. Hell, I'd already double-crossed the most powerful woman in Fairwood and now I harbored her very much *not* murdered stepson.

How the fuck did I think this was a good idea?

My personal phone buzzed with a notification that a very nice chunk of cash had been deposited in my account seconds before the burner phone binged with a text from Hilary's number.

Hilary: There's your money. Now send me the proof if you want the rest.

fairestofthemallHGDeWitt@fairwoodmail.com

This bitch was unbelievable. Ten bucks said I could hack into her accounts within twenty minutes and wipe her out—and I wasn't even an accomplished hacker. But I'd keep that information in the back of my mind for future use.

Checking to be sure I was in the VPN on my burner, I opened one of several fake email accounts and sent the Photoshopped image of Zane. My contact had done an amazing job with the quick snapshot I'd sent him of Zane laid out in bed earlier. The resulting image he'd provided looked very much like a deceased body with his heart carved out of his chest—just like step-mommy dearest had requested.

I called Hilary back. "Check your email for proof number one." Checking my watch, I grinned. "And proof number two should be arriving at your doorstep any moment now."

"What? What is it?"

I heard the doorbell ring in the background. "Better go check."

Hilary cursed but I heard rustling and the door opening. "It's a box."

"Open it."

I heard her gasp and the clunk of the ornate wooden box I'd requested be delivered. "You sick fuck."

Chuckling, I leaned back on the bench and enjoyed the late-fall sunshine on my face. "I'm not the one who hired a hitman to carve her stepson's heart from his chest, am I?"

"I didn't say deliver it to my door."

"Consider it a personal touch of my services. Now, I expect my money within two minutes. And don't ever contact me again. This is done, never happened, and we'll hopefully never cross paths." I hung up, stood, and dropped the phone to the hard asphalt. Crushing it with my big, black boot, I bent to pick up the pieces. Depositing the various chunks of the phone into a small brook, a trashcan, and a dumpster next to the playground, I made my way back to The Woods.

As I walked, a notification buzzed. Hilary had paid the rest of the blood money.

I grinned.

Now, all I had to do was keep Zane safe.

It was likely stupid to think I could hide him in plain sight and keep Hilary from finding out the truth.

But something about that kid had me contemplating stupid things.

A lot of stupid things.

"Wait, are you saying Hilary DeWitt—the woman who owns and controls most of Fairwood—hired you to kill her stepson?" A frown upon his face, Aiden was in a perpetually bad mood—only Felix seemed to be able to get smiles and blushes from the man.

"Um, can we back up to the part where Holter kills people for money?" Felix asked.

"I don't kill people for money—"

"You do it for free?" Dodie asked, his eyes wide.

Running a hand over my face, I took a deep breath. "We need to wake up Zane, but I wanted to give you all a little background. I've never trusted anyone to know my story and the fact I'm telling seven people all at once is a bit overwhelming."

Lorien put a hand on my shoulder just as Swayze sneezed and turned away slightly to shoot some sort of mist up his nose. "We appreciate the trust, and learning more about you," Lorien said.

Another deep breath.

"I don't stay in one place for long. Signing on with you for nine months is the most committed I've ever been to a place since my mom kicked me out." I shot a look at the group when I sensed questions about that. Now wasn't the time. I'd never shared anything about my past with others. "I do a lot of jobs. Officially, I'm a bounty hunter—pretty much off-the-books type stuff."

"Unofficially?" Concord asked.

"I'm a hitman—but I mostly find people, make them pay, rough them up, or bring them in. It's not like I go around killing people weekly. And the people I'm looking for are the worst of the worst—" I paused and looked toward Zane's door. "Usually. Until this one. I found him and there wasn't a single cell in my body that thought he was bad. So, I made a split-second decision, brought him here, and faked his death."

"Hilary DeWitt paid you and thinks you killed her stepson?" Asa asked.

"Yeah," I answered on a sigh. "And I need to tell Zane and figure some shit out."

"If it hasn't already been said," Felix started, "he's welcome here for as long as needed."

"You haven't even met him." I narrowed my eyes. Who were these guys and how had I ended up with them?

Felix shrugged. "We trust each other. When Asa brought you in, none of us questioned it."

"You should have questioned it."

He shook his head. "No, we trust each other."

"And now we trust you," Concord added.

"If you say this kid is legit, we believe you," Swayze said.

"You're all off your fucking rockers," I growled, but something warm and weird spread through my chest.

They all smiled.

"But I appreciate the trust. I'll try not to fuck it up."

Felix slapped me on the back. "Let's meet Zane and see what his thoughts are."

CHAPTER 6
ZANE

"If he stays, are you?" The soft voice outside my door tapped at my consciousness.

"There's still a lot of the nine months left." That voice belonged to Holter. The big man could have been scary, but something about him brought me comfort. "Not even sure he'll want to stay." A pause. "But yeah, somewhere between that evil witch calling, finding him, and now, I guess I've decided I'll at least stick around for the nine months."

"You're welcome here much longer than that," another voice offered.

I tried to picture the men outside my door. In the past, knowing unknown people were possibly getting ready to enter my room would have had me teetering between panic and shutting myself off from the impending pain.

But Holter had locked my door. I was safe.

Shifting slightly, I rolled to a sitting position and assessed my body.

Stiff and achy. Definitely some sore spots. But nothing that would kill me.

And for the first time since Hilary started trafficking me, I didn't have the niggling voice at the back of my head whispering it would be better off if I died. Something about this place and the people—at least Holter and Asa, so far—had me looking forward to the future.

That, and the deep, driving desire to pay back all the pieces of shit who ever bought and used me.

And kill Hilary.

Obviously.

I pulled myself up and headed to the bathroom. After a quick piss—grateful not to see blood—I washed my face gently to avoid the worst of the scrapes and bruises. As I walked out of the bathroom, a soft knock sounded at the door connecting to Holter's room.

"Zane?" Holter said from the other side. "Zane? You awake?"

"Yeah," I answered.

"Can you get the door?"

I moved gingerly to the back corner and opened the door. "Hey."

"How do you feel?"

"Better. I'll heal."

"Ready to meet the guys?"

"All seven of them?"

Holter winced and a pretty blush filled his face. "Yeah. But they really aren't overwhelming. Aiden is the only one who can come across a bit grumpy, but Felix keeps him grounded."

"And you'll tell me what you know about Hilary?"

Holter nodded.

"Can I come out of my room?"

Frown lines marred his forehead. "Of course. You weren't locked in here to keep you prisoner, just for your own comfort level. You can come and go as you please."

At a base-level, I'd known that, but hearing him say it —knowing I was no longer Hilary's prisoner, her pawn, her piece of meat she sold to the highest bidder—sent a thrill racing through me.

I'd done what I had to do to protect the children and keep my dad's name clear. But now, it was my time. Hilary and her clients would pay. I'd be allowed to start living my life. The DeWitt name would be safe. And the children wouldn't be in danger.

Instead of going out the main door of my room, I followed Holter through the connecting door. His room was identical to mine and made me wonder if this place had originally been a hotel or a dorm or something similar.

Holter's space was bare. The bed was rumpled and unmade. Nothing in the room made it *his*. Glancing toward his bathroom, I saw a few bottles on the vanity.

"Love the décor," I deadpanned.

Holter shot me a look. "I've only been here a couple months. I'm not planning on staying and I'm not a big decorator. I don't stay long enough to make a place mine."

Hmmm, that would need to be explored.

If Holter and I were to be friends.

I eyed him.

Friends or more.

Or both.

And I had a feeling we were.

Going to be both.

If I got my way.

And for the first time since my father died, I was in a position to get my way.

I'd just had to hope Holter agreed.

Walking into the living room, I came up short. Seven extremely attractive men sat on a large L-shaped couch, a loveseat, and two recliners.

One looked up from his phone with a smile. "Figured we might want pizza." He blushed. "Well, *I* want pizza. What do you want on yours? Anything you don't like?"

Holter's large hand brushed gently over my lower back—the touch offering comfort, not the usual panic when someone was too close, but something else also zinged through my blood. "That's Concord. He's a therapist."

"If you're living here for a bit, I can't offer my services," Concord said, "but I can suggest some really good therapists if you think it's something you might be interested in."

Therapy.

Talking to someone about the hell I'd been through.

Yeah, it was probably a good idea.

But the thought terrified me.

Before I could say anything, someone spoke up.

"I'll take pizza," a man with a slightly red nose and watery eyes said as he gazed adoringly at Concord. "'Bout the only thing I'm *not* allergic to."

Holter continued. "That's Swayze. Terrible allergies. He's a landscaper."

"Zane?" Concord asked.

"Oh, um, pepperoni is good."

"Gotcha. Holter, what do you want?"

"I'm easy, get whatever," Holter answered. Then he pointed toward the other men. "That's Lorien. He's a massage therapist and acupuncturist."

"I specialize in sleep disorders," Lorien said.

My stomach took that exact moment to grumble loudly.

"God, we're terrible hosts," one of the men said, jumping to his feet. "We've got food to hold you over until the pizza gets here. Banana? Apple? Orange? Crackers?"

"Apple, please," I answered automatically.

"That's Felix. He's the sunshine of the grumpy sunshine couple," Holter explained as he guided me to sit on the couch. "He and Aiden," he paused as the man Felix had been sitting next to on the loveseat nodded a greeting if not a smile, "own 7—that's a bar in town where some of us work."

Felix returned and handed me the most gorgeous, shiny apple. My mouth immediately watered and I took the fruit gratefully. Biting into the crisp, sweet flesh, I nearly cried. Hilary banned apples when I returned home around age twelve because she knew I loved them. It was one more way she lorded her power over me.

"You like apples, huh?" a big guy with a dopey smile asked. "Me too. Pretty much any fruit. Love it."

"That's Dodie. Real name is Dwayne Dodieu—"

"But do I look like a Dwayne? Nah, Dodie fits me just fine," the man, Dodie, finished for Holter.

"And you already met Asa," Holter said.

"So, that's the whole crew," Felix said with a grin. "This," he gestured around the room, "is The Woods. We own the building and live here. If you know the area, it's not much to look at on the outside, but we think it's pretty nice on the inside."

"It's great," I said around a bite of apple. "Thank you for letting me come here."

"You know about us, tell us about you," Aiden demanded, that perpetual frown going strong.

"What Aiden means to say in a much nicer way," Felix intervened, "is we'd like to know more about you if you're comfortable telling us."

"That's what I said," Aiden grumped.

"Sure it is, babe." Felix leaned over and kissed Aiden's cheek.

The rest of the crew smiled.

"Zane DeWitt. Bad shit in my past, but I'm out now. I need a job, a place to stay, and time to plan revenge." I took another bite of the apple. "Oh," my words garbled slightly, "and I'm going to kill Hilary Grimstead."

Eight pairs of eyes froze on me in various forms of surprise.

I shrugged. "I don't mean to drag you into my shit—it's probably best if I leave as quickly as I can get my own clothes back." Gesturing to the borrowed clothes, I went on. "Thanks for these by the way. But you don't want to be a part of my mess. I'm sure of that. So, the less I tell you, the better." I ate the rest of the apple, loving the crunch and cool, sweet flavor on my tongue. "I don't have access to my money right this second, but I can get you some cash for my part of the pizza if you'll let me grab a few bites before changing my clothes and heading out."

Holter cleared his throat and the other seven men glanced back and forth between him and each other.

"Nah," Aiden said, crossing his arms over his chest. "You've got us intrigued. And we work together as a group." His gaze traveled around the group once again and I saw almost imperceptible nods from each man. "You're one of us if you want to be. We won't force you, but we've always known we were waiting for two more people to fill these rooms. When Holter came to town, we knew he was a good fit."

"Even if he's still not sure of it," Felix said with a smile.

Holter huffed and rolled his eyes, but I saw a smile tug at his pretty lips.

"And now you."

I narrowed my eyes. "I just told you I've got a ton of shit in my past and I plan on killing the most powerful woman in Fairwood. Why would you want me to stay here?"

Concord and Swayze leaned closer to each other.

Dodie blushed when Asa gave him a wink.

Lorien closed his eyes in a look of complete peace.

Felix put an arm around Aiden's shoulders.

"We're all kinda underdogs in our own right," Aiden said. "Not like we're fragile or weak, but we know what it's like to have a past, to struggle, to overcome." He shrugged. "We recognize our own. If you have reason to kill Hilary Grimstead, we'll stand by you. She's the worst type of person—corrupt, using her power against people; she's evil personified—none of us would shed a tear to see her gone from town."

I wasn't sure what to make of the men and their easy, welcoming support of me—someone they'd just barely met. "Hilary is my main focus, but there are several others I plan to make pay." My words were a warning, meant to steer them away from this crazy idea to bring me into their fold.

"Do those others have anything to do with the injuries I saw?" Asa asked.

I nodded.

"The ones he couldn't see?" Holter asked, his warm hand heavier against my back.

Swallowing thickly and pushing memories away, I nodded again.

"Then the offer remains," Felix said. "Holter here is still getting used to us—and us to him—but he's a resourceful guy. The rest of us have our talents and skills —hidden and otherwise. We're ready and willing."

The doorbell sounded.

Dodie jumped up and made his way to grab the pizzas.

Soon, the entire space filled with the spicy, savory aroma of sauce, cheese, and toppings. For a moment, the invitation to stay was forgotten and we filled our bellies.

I mostly just listened to the others chat about their jobs, random happenings, and each other.

Holter stayed pretty quiet; joining the conversation only when asked a direct question or if he had something to add. He appeared to be a fairly stoic and quiet guy—it made sense he wasn't super chummy with the group if he hadn't been there that long.

When the pizza was pretty much demolished, Aiden checked his watch. "We've still got a bit of time before some of us need to head to work. Tell us as much or as little as you're comfortable sharing." Felix beamed at his partner. Probably for asking in a nicer way. They were actually really cute together.

Seated on the chaise lounge part of the couch, Holter beside me, I rubbed clammy hands down my thighs. For some reason, the close, warm presence of his large body next to mine spurred me on. And the eight pairs of eyes watching me—no judgement, no bad intentions, just curiosity and a willingness to help—spoke volumes.

"I don't want to get too graphic." My voice wavered. I took a deep breath and just focused on the way Holter's hand immediately went to my back in a show of protection and support. "My mom died when I was very young."

A smile ghosted over my lips. I had wonderful memories of my parents, especially those from before my mother died. I honestly thought having my family together during my most formative years was one of the reasons I hadn't completely lost myself to the heartache, pain, and trauma I'd been dealt.

"My dad ended up marrying Hilary Grimstead. He

was lost in grief and thought he was doing what was best for me—giving me a mother—I know that now. And she played him good. Slowly, but surely, she got him to trust her, believe her, and quietly moved some of her own people into the staff positions. I think his grief was too much and he let the pain overtake him. I'm one hundred percent sure she killed him. He wasn't healthy ever since my mom died, but I know Hilary made sure he went quicker. She's an evil cunt and I swear she's got some kind of dark magic in her because the way she can manipulate and sway people is beyond wicked."

I held my head in my hands and breathed deeply.

"When my dad was getting sicker, he didn't want me to witness the death of another parent—even though, I barely remember anything about my mom's death other than being sad she was there one day and then she wasn't. So, he sent me to a boarding school. It was nice. I had friends even though I was quiet. I liked my studies. And I liked being away from Hilary. My dad had been gone a while when she sent for me. She made me come back to Fairwood when I was twelve. I was terrified, but she mostly left me alone. She just did petty shit like banning apples from the house because she knew they were my favorite. And forcing me to look in mirrors with her and tell her she was prettier than me—like, she'd do the whole 'Mirror, mirror, on the wall, who's the prettiest of them all?' and then make me say she was the prettiest and I was ugly. Weird shit like that—got really old—but things were mostly okay."

The entire room hung on my every word.

Holter's thumb rubbed gentle circles on the small of my back.

That was weird, right? It was completely ridiculous that I liked his touch and wanted to lean into him, let him support me.

Thoughts for another time.

"Until it wasn't," I said in a rush, the sick pain of what she put me through rising in my throat. "She trafficked me. Kept me locked up for a while—sent buyers to my room to do whatever sick, twisted things they wanted." I scoffed. "As if sexually assaulting a kid isn't sick and twisted enough, these people got off even more on the worst of the worst." I took a calming breath through my nose in hopes of quelling the nausea. "For a few years, the buyers were mostly interested in the fight I put up and Hilary marketed me that way."

I hated the pity I saw in the men's eyes, but the rage I also saw there gave me hope.

"Once she knew she had me where she wanted me..." I paused and swallowed down the sick fear I had for those kids going through what I went through, "she told me she'd traffic the kids at the DeWitt Children's Home—she would have had the means—and ruin my dad's name by convincing everyone he was a pedophile who set up the home for his own sick pleasure."

Holter tensed beside me and horror mixed with the rage filled the faces of the men around me.

"Anyway, once she had me in a position where she didn't have to keep me captive—I agreed to the situation as long as she left the kids alone—she sold me to anyone and everyone who wanted a piece—but she lost a few buyers who wanted more of a fight from me. I just wasn't giving that anymore. I finally made my peace with it—as much as one can make peace with being trafficked and assaulted by some of the most influential names in the city—and accepted my fate for the time remaining. The less I fought, the easier it was to slip into the darkness of my mind and block out the pain. I'm fucked up when it comes to sex, arousal, intimacy, all of that." My cheeks heated—I wanted so much in that area of my life, but it would take time and someone special to help me find it. "But that's for a different time."

The men cleared their throats and I worried I'd said too much.

Eventually, someone spoke.

"So, what was different about today?" Swayze asked.

I drew in a deep breath. I caught Concord watching me and I knew he couldn't help but have his therapist hat on. I didn't really like sitting there being analyzed, but I didn't get the feeling he was doing it to judge me—hell, I doubted he could even turn it off. I kinda wanted to ask him for his input, but he'd already said he couldn't offer his services if I was going to live with them.

Was I?

Going to live with them?

I shook off the question.

"She knew I'd leave at twenty-five." I shrugged. "I'm twenty-five and I headed to the bank to get things set up for my inheritance from my dad. Her goons jumped me. They didn't leave me for dead, so I'm not exactly sure what her plan was, but I know she *wanted* me dead."

I glanced at Holter and he nodded. "That's where I come in."

My stomach churned, but I waited.

"Hilary contacted me and said she wanted to hire me."

"For?" I asked.

Holter hesitated.

"He needs to know it all," Felix urged.

"I'm a bounty hunter mostly, but I've been known to act as a hitman." Holter's eyes caught mine and held, boring deep.

"She hired you to kill me?" I whispered.

He nodded.

"Why didn't you?"

Holter shook his head. "I couldn't do it. The only people I've ever killed have been the scum of the earth. I found you huddled on the ground in that alley and I knew I was on the wrong side of the situation."

Relief and gratitude rushed through me. "Thank you," I whispered. "As many times as I closed my eyes and tried to block out the pain, sometimes wondering if I'd just be better off dead, I'd rather live and carry out my revenge." Of its own accord, my hand traveled to Holter's thick thigh. "Thank you for letting me live."

The room was silent.

"But what happened when you told her you weren't taking the job?" I asked.

Holter's jaw tightened. "I didn't tell her that."

For one split-second, I worried maybe I'd misread him and he was actually dangerous, but then I saw the determination and rage in his eyes. "What did you tell her?"

"First, that she was a moron for using her real name and cell phone. Second, I demanded half the payment for me to send her pictures of you looking very much dead. Then I delivered your heart to her doorstep. She pretended not to be happy about it, but that narcissistic bitch couldn't help but be thrilled to know you were gone. She paid the second half. I told her to never contact me again and destroyed the burner phone." He waved a phone around.

Now it was Holter's turn to have every pair of eyes glued to him in shock and horror.

"I'm sorry, you did *what*?" I asked.

"Oh my god, you didn't kill someone else to fake her out, did you?" Dodie asked.

"Photoshop and pig's heart. I paid someone to doctor a photo of you to look very much dead and missing your heart. I paid someone else to deliver a pig's heart to her door in a very fancy box."

"What? Why?" Swayze asked.

Holter shrugged. "Pig's hearts are very close in structure to human hearts. She's evil as hell, but I doubt she's going to dissect a bloody organ to be sure it's human."

The guys kept looking at him.

"What? This is why I told you all I don't stick around and you shouldn't trust me."

"No, no," Asa said. "It's okay. I think we all just need a moment to let it sink in. Both of you. There's *a lot* of details to take in."

"And maybe you could stop changing phones like some people change their socks?" Aiden asked. "Just when I think I have your number in my contacts right, you fuckin' change it."

Holter's cheeks pinked. "Sorry. I've never had a group of friends before, no one to ever share my actual contact information with. I'm used to just using burner phones and coming and going as I please."

"You can come and go as you please," Felix said. "Just know that you have people who care about you. If you're comfortable with giving us your number, we'll keep it safe."

Holter looked as if he was making a life or death decision, but he finally nodded. "Yeah, I can do that. But it's just between us, yeah?"

Everyone nodded, me included.

I guess I had decided I was okay with being a part of The Woods crew.

"And don't be surprised if I sometimes still use the burner phones," Holter said. "It's habit."

"Is Holter even your real name?" Lorien asked gently.

"Yeah," Holter answered. "But it's not Holter Jones. It's Holter Todd. You're the only people aside from my mother who know my legal name." He clenched his jaw. "Please don't make me regret that."

Despite not trusting anyone since my mom and dad, I knew without a doubt that this group of men could be trusted.

"So, what's the plan?" Dodie asked, clapping his hands together like he was ready for some excitement.

"We've got some openings at 7," Felix said.

Aiden shot him a look.

"What?" Felix grinned. "We do."

"It's not like he's got experience. Plus, he probably doesn't want a bunch of men leering at him all night." Aiden threw me a somewhat apologetic look.

"What's the job?" I asked.

"We need someone who can tend the bar and take part in the drag shows as needed," Felix said.

"There's security at the bar?"

Aiden nodded. "The best. Dodie and Holter are part of the team."

"I'm a fast learner. Some of my friends from school and I used to mix drinks in their parents' well-stocked bars. We'd look up recipes and try them out." I scowled at the memory, wondering what my friends thought when I pretty much dropped from the face of the earth. What did Hilary say to explain that away? "I can definitely do the bar."

"And drag?" Felix asked. "It's not a requirement, but it would give you more hours."

Running a hand through my ink-black hair, I said, "I've dressed in drag before. I like doing my makeup and becoming someone else. One of the highest-paying buyers caught me in drag once. Totally got off on it. Beat the shit out of me for making him like it so much," I recalled, the pain of that night still vivid in my mind. "He was a real closet-case. Blamed me every time he got off doing something with me because he wasn't gay or whatever. Blah, blah, blah. The vast majority of the men who got off doing things to me swore they weren't gay and hurt me worse when they liked it." I shook my head, pulling myself from the memories. “Anyway, yeah, I can do drag. I’m a good dancer. I like to pretend I’m someone else.”

“It’s actually a good idea,” Dodie said.

We looked at him.

“I mean, it’s a good disguise. A lot of times when the queens are all dressed up and have their makeup on, I wouldn’t even recognize them if I didn’t *know* them. If Hilary or her cronies come looking for Zane for some reason, drag is a good way to hide in plain sight.”

Everyone nodded.

“Dodie’s right,” Holter said. “And working at the bar keeps you around one of us at pretty much all times.” He glanced my way. “I know being told what to do and not having freedom is a thing for you, but would you consider agreeing to one of us being with you any time you leave The Woods?”

I glanced around the large, open living room at the eight men who had immediately welcomed me into their fold and jumped at the chance to help protect me and take down Hilary. “Yeah, that’s probably the safest bet.”

So, it was decided.

I’d hide in plain sight. Hilary likely wouldn’t be looking for me for a while; she thought I was dead, so I had some time before I had to worry about her coming after me.

It wouldn’t last forever, but we had a bit of cushion now. And when she realized I wasn’t dead, we’d be ready.

Holter gave me a phone I could use as my own since Hilary’s men took my phone when they dumped me.

I'd get my money. She had no access to my inheritance and, if I had to, I'd contact my father's attorney and get the money set up through a bank outside of Fairwood. I wasn't sure how Holter got it done, but he assured me my attorney had been contacted, sworn to secrecy about my supposed death, and was to have absolutely no contact with Hilary regarding me.

I'd learn to work behind the bar and join the drag show at 7.

I wouldn't go anywhere without one of the guys.

And we'd work our way toward taking out Hilary and her clients in order to save any others from the evil cunt.

CHAPTER 7
HOLTER

"I'm worried about the kids at the home," Zane said as he leaned into the mirror to apply mascara. He'd dressed in the short skirt, silky tank, and heels Dodie and Asa had purchased earlier, and was now putting the final touches on his makeup before I walked him to 7.

He'd insisted he felt well enough to go see the bar and argued he didn't want to be at home while we were at work. Asa had agreed Zane was in good enough shape to go out, as long as he listened to his body and took it easy.

"I know she's always had the means to traffic them—just because she told me she wouldn't doesn't mean she didn't—but now that I'm no longer in the picture, I'm scared for them."

"I'll make some calls. The connections I have are part of a very large network of people; maybe they can get some eyes on the inside and offer some protection."

Zane's deep brown eyes met mine in the mirror and he smiled. "Thank you."

His whisper warmed my heart and any thought I had of saving this kid and walking away flew out the window. I was drawn to him like a moth to a flame.

And I was willing to burn.

He tossed the mascara back into the bag of cosmetics Dodie and Asa had bought him and studied himself in the mirror. "Do I look hot?"

"I thought the point was to disguise yourself."

"Can't I look hot while doing it?" He blew me a kiss.

I grunted.

Turning from the mirror, Zane sauntered over to me. "Do. I. Look. Hot?" He poked a finger to my chest.

"You know you're hot," I muttered.

"Yeah," his demeanor switched from flirty to unsure and sad, "but the only people who have ever thought I was hot were people paying for the chance to hurt me. I just—"

I cut him off, tipping up his chin, loving the little gasp of surprise escaping his blood-red lips. "You're the prettiest, hottest, most gorgeous man I've ever seen." That close, I smelled mint toothpaste on his breath. The scent of soap and hair product mixed with his body heat to tickle my nose. "Happy?"

Zane's big brown eyes blinked up at me and he nodded.

"Good. Let's go. I don't want to be late for my shift." Working at 7 was something I'd sworn I didn't want to do—didn't *need* to do—but I found myself enjoying the job more and more. Maybe because it was never boring.

Maybe because it got me out among people. Maybe because it meant I got to spend time with Dodie, Felix, and Aiden—and the other guys when they came in for drinks. Either way, I didn't *like* that I enjoyed the job, but that didn't stop me from looking forward to my shifts.

And now I'd gone and assigned myself to be Zane's personal shadow when what I really should have done was left town the moment I knew he was safe at The Woods.

Instead, I followed him out the door and tried my best not to focus on how perfect his ass looked in the tight skirt. How kissable his porcelain skin looked under the street lights. How ridiculously hot he looked in the black wig.

No.

Zane was gorgeous and something deep inside of me was drawn to him like nothing I'd ever known.

But he had a traumatic past.

I had a traumatic past.

Mixing those things together was a recipe for disaster.

Or maybe you can help each other heal.

"You're gay, right?" Zane asked as we headed toward 7. The night was nice and the bar wasn't far.

"Something like that."

He cocked a brow and waited.

"I've been with women and men. Women when I was younger and trying to prove something—trying to run from it all, trying to make my future better than my present at that time."

"But?"

I shrugged. "But I'm into guys. Not like relationship-wise—that's not something I do—but sexually, yeah."

Zane gave me a cute little grin. "Good to know."

What was going through this kid's head? He'd been hurt. Badly. I guess his past didn't mean he couldn't find someone attractive and bring out the flirty side.

But he was doing it with the wrong guy.

Whatever. You know you'd take him home and bend him over in a heartbeat.

No.

I needed to get that shit out of my head. Zane had been hurt and needed someone a lot more sensitive and caring than me.

Didn't mean the image of him under me was one I could push away easily, but I knew getting involved with Zane beyond protecting him was a line I just shouldn't cross.

No matter how delicious he looked swaying his hips as we approached 7 and walked through the outer door.

Dodie's eyes lit up when he saw us coming. "There they are." The guy was a goof, but he was one of the most genuine people I'd ever met. I wasn't upset about having Dodie on my side.

The big dope whistled as he checked out Zane.

And I bit back the growl trying to escape my chest.

What the fuck?

I didn't have any claim to Zane. Even if I *wanted* to stake a claim—which I didn't—I knew damn well it wasn't a good idea. Plus, Dodie was just being Dodie. He was one hundred percent hung up on Asa, no doubt about that. There was absolutely no reason for my chest to clench in the green fist of jealousy when a guy I considered my friend whistled at the guy I most definitely wasn't involved with.

And would *not* get involved with.

Zane's cheeks blushed and he hooked his arm through mine. "Think it's a good enough disguise?"

I didn't mind Zane holding onto me. Sure, it was likely just because he felt safe with me—something I doubted he'd ever really felt with anyone else since losing his dad—but that didn't stop the warm flush working its way from my chest to my neck.

Fuck.

I didn't need to add *blushing* to the list of ways Zane affected me.

"For sure." Dodie nodded, his big, innocent eyes wide. "Unless she has some sort of facial recognition software or some shit, she wouldn't recognize you right away. And once you're in drag for the show, the makeup will hide you even more." He paused and listened to something in the radio earbud he wore. With a big smile, he gestured over his shoulder. "Felix wants us inside."

"It's not even time to open yet." I'd been hoping I'd have time to show Zane around and get him a bit more comfortable with the place before the doors opened. I knew he'd be fairly safe inside 7; our security was good. But that didn't mean I wanted to throw him to the wolves right away.

Dodie bit his lip, trying to hide his big goofy smile. "Just something he wants to...um...talk about before starting time. To you both. And me."

I narrowed my eyes at him. "Ohh-kay," I drawled. Dodie was a dope, totally lovable, and a terrible liar.

The bar was quiet, dark, and cool when we entered.

7 had been named after the seven friends who owned The Woods and was *the* top bar in Fairwood. While 7 wasn't advertised as a gay bar, it was well-known in town as a safe and welcoming place for queer folks to have fun. Non-queer groups sometimes made the rounds, stopping in 7 as they bar-hopped through Fairwood, and they were welcome—as long as they adhered to the rules and treated people with dignity and respect.

Felix and Aiden ran 7. Dodie was part of their security team. The rest of the guys were part owners; more silent financial partners than hands-on, although, Swayze *did* take care of the landscaping. And all of the guys had played a part in renovating the inside and designing the aesthetic of the place.

The crew had opted to decorate the bar and club based on the seven precious gemstones—diamond, pearl, ruby, sapphire, emerald, oriental cat's-eye, and alexandrite. Since the majority of the seven precious gemstones were mined from the earth, Felix had suggested they make the main bar area look like an underground mine. From that point on, the décor basically designed itself from what the guys had told me.

The bar and dining area were dark and lit with lanterns reminiscent of an underground mine. The tables and chairs were all iron and wood that gave the feel of mine carts, rails, and stone picks.

There were three stages. The small stage to the left

was cat's-eye and boasted honey-golds and the easily-recognizable cat's-eye stones.

The stage to the right was alexandrite. They'd set up the lighting so the stage's decorations changed from green to a purple-ish red depending on which light shone on it.

The middle stage was pearl. A large clam shell took up the whole width and it was where the performers walked through pearlescent streamers as they took the stage. Fake bubbles and pearl garland finished off the main stage.

There were four separate areas taking up both sides of the stage for private parties and groups who didn't want to watch the entertainment. The diamond room glittered and reflected the many colors of the space. The ruby room was obviously a deep, dark red with red velvet couches. The emerald room reminded me of the Wizard of Oz as it glowed a brilliant green. And the sapphire room sparkled in cool, vibrant blue.

I hadn't been there long, but newcomers always commented on the unique and gorgeous interior. Regulars often noted the ambiance was one part that kept them coming back.

Felix and Aiden could have stopped with the 7 theme after the seven precious gemstones used to decorate the place, but they didn't. They definitely went all out.

7's mission was to embrace seven main core values:

Patrons of 7 will always receive the best in entertainment, food, dessert, drinks, vibe, safety, and that found-family feeling. If ever you feel as if one of these is missing or not up to par, please let us know.

Within their mission, Aiden had pushed for keeping up with the seven vibe.

Seven *main* foods along with a rotation of specialties.

Seven desserts which their kitchen circulated throughout the month.

Seven signature drinks in addition to local beers, ciders, liquors, and a variety of non-alcoholic choices.

The seven signature drinks, of course, were named after the group of friends.

The Felix- a whiskey sour.

The Aiden- a vodka gimlet.

The Dodie- a Tom Collins.

The Asa- a gin martini.

The Swayze- a Moscow mule.

The Concord- a Cosmopolitan.

The Lorien- a strawberry mojito.

One Sunday a month, 7 hosted a brunch with a drink menu featuring the always-popular mimosa, mint julep, sangria, Long Island iced tea, and Bloody Mary. The brunch menu boasted sweet and savory items such as blueberry-lemon ricotta stuffed French toast, breakfast tostadas, a make-your-own waffle bar, spinach and cheese quiche, coffee cake, bagels, crepes, and breakfast sandwiches.

The guys had really done something special with 7 and it was somewhere people could go for the best food, drinks, entertainment, and safety.

If I was someone looking for a place like 7, I definitely would have considered it a diamond in the rough and been grateful for the welcoming atmosphere and the found-family vibe.

I wasn't that type of person, obviously, but it was easy to see why others liked the place.

For me, it was a job.

Plain and simple.

Maybe you shouldn't let yourself get too tied up in the place if you think you're going to be leaving.

I pushed the thought away. Whether I was leaving or not didn't mean I couldn't enjoy my new job and the friends I was making.

Pulling me from the mess my head was in, the lights came on in one blinding click. The whole crew merged into the dining area singing Happy Birthday as Felix beamed as bright as the candles on the enormous cake he carried toward us.

Zane gripped my arm tightly and turned his gorgeous smile up to look at me. "Did you plan this?"

I shook my head, suddenly wishing I *had* been thoughtful enough to make it happen. "Not me. But happy birthday, princess."

He wrinkled his nose and narrowed his eyes, but even the nickname he didn't love couldn't keep the smile off his face.

As the song finished and Felix placed the cake on the table, the guys whooped and cheered.

A large sheet cake decorated with rainbow icing and the words *Happy Birthday, Zane* lay before us. As Felix lit the final candles shaped as a 2 and a 5, Zane beamed and whispered, "Thank you. No one has given me a birthday party since the last few my dad remembered to plan after my mom died."

God.

This kid.

I wanted to wrap him in my arms and hold him close until all the bad shit went away. I knew from experience, traumatic pasts didn't work that way, but that didn't keep me from wishing it was something I could do.

For the next hour, the guys welcomed Zane into their fold even more quickly and warmly than they'd welcomed me. They weren't pushovers—I'd seen them all shut out people at the bar who wanted to step into The Woods crew—but they clearly saw the same thing in Zane as I did. There was a magic about him that made all of us want to be close to him, to protect him, and to help him fight his demons.

I couldn't help the thought that Zane had been brought into my life—and theirs—for reasons we didn't quite understand. Even the fact that I'd randomly stopped in Fairwood and accidentally discovered the guys, The Woods, and 7 had me wondering just what fate was up to.

By the time 7 opened, we had a plan. Zane would shadow the current bartender for a while—Sammy was good, but he needed to cut back his hours because his partner was having a baby and he was starting classes at the local college. As Zane took on the bar, he'd also watch the resident drag queens who performed regularly, as well as the locals who stopped by to perform as the mood struck.

Once Zane had the bartending down, he'd start performing if he was comfortable with it.

"That gives me time to come up with some stage

outfits." Zane licked a smear of icing from the corner of his lips. "Can I wear whatever I want behind the bar?"

"Have to have a name tag and one piece of clothing should have our logo on it," Aiden said. He frowned. "If we're trying to keep you under that bitch's radar, we probably shouldn't use your real name. What's Zane mean?"

Zane's cheeks pinked. "My dad used to tell me my mom had some sort of premonition about me being born with blood-red lips, hair black as the raven's, and skin as white as snow. Since DeWitt means *white*, she looked for names that meant *snow*. She found Zane and decided it was perfect." He shrugged, rolling his eyes, but I could tell the story brought him good memories of his parents. "So, I'm basically Snow White."

Aiden nodded. "That's kinda cool. How about you just go by Snow when you're behind the bar. People won't really know if it's a nickname or a last name or whatever. And you'll be dressed up and in makeup, so you should be fairly anonymous."

"You're welcome to check out the catalog where we order our uniforms and see if there's something that works for what you're wanting," Felix offered. "You can get whatever name you want put on most everything."

"Perfect." Zane's deep brown eyes glowed with excitement.

~

Over the next couple months, Zane and I spent nearly every waking second together. I was his shadow—for protection reasons, of course. He was my shadow—for reasons I couldn't quite grasp.

Don't lie to yourself. You know damn well you both appreciate the company and enjoy spending time together. You totally have the hots for each other. Plus, he's interesting, sweet, and easy to talk to.

"Shut up," I muttered to myself as I turned off the shower after work one night.

I didn't usually make it a habit to *get to know* people—in fact, I avoided it whenever possible. *People* in my past had made me wary of anything to do with loving or trusting.

But I'd be damned if I hadn't gone and let Zane wedge himself into my life. Not like I loved the guy or anything like that. But he was a damn little worm inching his way into my thoughts and making me want to know more about him.

The good and the bad.

He'd taken the last couple months to recover and regroup. The kid had a shit-ton of healing to do—trauma like he'd gone through wasn't something that just went away. Although, I had to say he was already making strides with the therapist Concord had set him up with.

Zane had wanted to pounce on Hilary and her clients as soon as possible. Once I'd assured him I had some people inside the children's home watching and preventing any of the kids from being hurt, he'd agreed to pausing long enough to gather information and make a plan.

We needed to be ready in case Hilary figured out he wasn't dead sooner than I assumed she would. Best case, she'd never figure it out. I wasn't counting on that, but she *was* narcissistic enough to think only of herself and never realize her stepson was alive. Worst case, she figured it out much sooner than any of us thought she would.

Either way, Zane had a ton of information against a very large number of people. He hadn't shared it with me yet. I wasn't sure he needed to give me the gory details. But I knew there were several people in Fairwood whose upper echelon of living would soon be coming to an end.

I wanted them all to pay for what they'd done to Zane.

For what they'd done to any number of victims. It wasn't reasonable to think they were buying *only* Zane. That was another reason I'd convinced him to hold off—I needed time for some of my contacts to dig deeper and find others who could help put Hilary and the buyers away. Or six feet under. I wasn't picky.

Pulling on a pair of boxers, I moved to the door connecting our rooms, smiling as I heard Zane singing in his bathroom.

How had I gone and gotten such a soft spot for him in such a short amount of time? Sure, he was gorgeous, but it was more than that. He nearly glowed with sweet goodness—his pain and his innocence a powerful mixture drawing me in. Plus, he was funny and smart.

And the way he devoured apples was the saddest and cutest thing ever. Seriously, the kid loved apples—probably ate two or three a day. Asa teased him that he was just trying to keep the doctor away, but we all knew Hilary had used the fruit to deprive and control him.

So, we bought apples by the bag and made sure he never went without.

Watching him as he gained freedom and started to heal was a privilege. I wasn't sure what I'd done to deserve it, but I appreciated it all the same.

Zane was rocking his new position behind the bar. He was a quick learner and the customers nearly knocked themselves out panting and drooling over him.

Not gonna lie, the kid looked good enough to eat as he mixed drinks. I felt like the Big Bad Wolf as I watched his perfect ass in short, silky, yellow booty shorts with the 7 logo across the ass. Blue ankle booties with laces crisscrossing all the way up his shapely calves and a red leather collar with his name in glitter finished off his outfit.

Outfit was a misnomer if you asked me.

Booty shorts, boots, and a collar weren't an *outfit*, but the customers loved it. Whether they drooled more over his sexy little ass, his long, lean legs, his flat belly with soft six-pack lines, or the hint of treasure trail between the shadows of that tantalizing V dipping beneath those silky shorts—or a deadly combination of all the above—there was no doubt in my mind that Zane brought in more drink orders, higher tips, and customers who stayed longer just to watch their favorite new bartender at work.

He left 7 grinning ear-to-ear every night, his bank account loaded down with tips from those adoring customers. He didn't *need* the money since he'd gotten everything squared away with the inheritance from his father—a task which had gotten much more in-depth since we needed to make sure Hilary didn't have any way of finding out he'd gotten the money. The contact I'd worked with made sure Zane's attorney had no contact with Hilary and was aware Zane was very much alive and ready to claim his inheritance.

I'd started looking forward to those trips we made home together each night. Despite a dark and disturbing past that had shaped the man he was today, Zane was one of the sweetest, most genuine, easy-to-like people I'd ever had the pleasure of knowing.

If I hadn't been looking ahead to the day I'd drive out of Fairwood for good, I knew I'd be tempted to consider Zane a friend. And maybe something more if I let him—but there was no way I was going there.

What would it hurt? A little fun with a guy you like? You've not liked *anyone in...*

Shutting down the thought, I crossed my arms over my chest and watched as Zane applied another layer of cream to his porcelain skin.

"You excited about tomorrow night?" I asked him from our connecting doorway. As usual, I'd walked him home from the bar when our shift ended. If I wasn't working and available to shadow him, one of the guys made sure Zane had a safe way home. But I'd slowly found myself making sure I was the one available to get him home safely.

Not sure what that was about.

And damn sure didn't want to dig into it.

We'd fallen into a habit of chatting together as we wound down from the bar—the door we shared between our rooms allowing for easy conversation. Our routines usually involved each of us taking a quick shower and slipping into pajamas—loose boxers for me and a big flowy t-shirt with booty shorts for him. Then Zane would tell me stories about mistakes he made mixing drinks or cheesy come-on lines from customers while I flossed, brushed my teeth, and took care of whatever hygiene tasks I needed to.

When Zane moved toward his own little bathroom, I'd take my place at the connecting door and tell him stories about terrible fake IDs, belligerent customers we had to turn away, and behind-the-scenes safety issues that no one else knew about if we were doing our job correctly. Zane watched me in the mirror, smiling and laughing at my words, as he brushed his teeth and performed a way-too-complicated-for-me nightly skincare routine.

My question stopped him short.

"Yes," he said, biting his lip, worry filling his big brown eyes. "But also super nervous."

"You've got the outfit and the songs. You've been practicing. I know you could do that routine in your sleep based on how many times you've run through it. Hell, *I* could probably do it in *my* sleep based on how many times I've heard those songs."

He giggled. "You haven't seen the whole thing, I wanted it to be a surprise for everyone."

"You'll be great. Everyone there is already a huge fan. Your biggest problem is going to be jealous queens pissed off you're stealing the spotlight from them."

"Oh, god." Zane's eyes widened. "Do you think they're going to be mad at me?"

"No one wants to have the spotlight taken away," I said. "There will likely be some catty behavior. But the queens I've met—the ones who are regulars at 7—are professionals and have their own following. The local girls who just pop in to perform as the mood strikes, they'll be more likely to get pissy." I shrugged. "But they all know Aiden and Felix don't put up with the drama and shit, so I don't think it will be a huge deal."

"I'm not planning on stealing the spotlight."

"Whatever." I moved to lean my back against the corner of the doorframe. Lifting my arms over my head for a deep stretch, I rubbed the hard angle into tight muscles with a groan. "You'll outshine them all."

Zane's eyes caught on my chest and my blood sizzled as he raked his gaze down to the waistband of my boxers.

And then lower.

Shit.

"You don't even know that I'll be good." Zane walked toward me, his teeth worrying that plump, red bottom lip.

"I guess we'll have to see. If you take to the stage as well as you've taken to the drinks, you'll bring down the house." I wasn't just blowing smoke up the guy's ass. He truly had caught on to the bartending gig quicker than anyone had expected him to. And I hadn't *seen* the whole routine, but based on the music, and the way Zane moved so gracefully in his daily life, I felt confident he was going to absolutely kill it with his performance.

Before I knew what was happening, Zane's slim, warm hand was pressed against my chest. Big, brown eyes blinked up at me.

"Whatcha doin', princess?" My words came out a lot breathier than intended. I'd been going for gruff and nonchalant. What I got was *this gorgeous man is about to bring me to my knees.*

"I like you, Holter," Zane said, his fingers sifting through my chest hair.

Clearing my throat, I took what I hoped would be more calming breath and less panting with desire. "I like you too."

Zane trailed his knuckles down my firm stomach, thumbing over my navel, and teasing fingertips along my waistband. "So, what are we gonna do about it?" Those big, glassy, brown eyes blinked up at me—wait a damned second—

I grabbed Zane's chin and turned his face for a better look at his eyes. Pupils blown. Glassy. Slow blinks.

Fuck.

"What did you take?" I growled.

Zane giggled. "Just something to make it fun. It's better when it doesn't hurt." He swallowed and blinked again. "Want to remember it if it's with you, but never done it without the drugs."

What.

The.

Fuck.

Images of my mom strung out on whatever substance she'd been able to get her hands on—or whatever shit her *boyfriend* of the moment had pumped her full of—giggling, nearly falling to the ground as she made her way to the bedroom behind him. Her distant eyes, full of pain and confusion when she'd see me watching. *"Go to your room, Holt. Be a good boy and just go."*

Fuck.

A fist squeezed my heart. My gut churned. Memories bombarded me. My mind waged a war over wanting to break down everything Zane had just said or shutting out all the shit and just taking him up on the offer.

The memories of my mom won out.

But his innocent eyes, so full of pain and desire and something else I couldn't quite name blinked rapidly, tears brimming.

"Look, princess," I said, brushing inky locks from his forehead. "I swore a long time ago I'd never take advantage of anyone under the influence."

"It's just easier this way." His words slurred slightly. "I wanna be with someone without the drugs, but I don't know how."

"Well, it won't be me. Not when you're high."

"It's okay, I took them by choice. Please?"

I shook my head. "No."

A single tear raced down his pale cheek. "Because I'm damaged goods? Because of what they did to me? I'm not sweet and innocent; I'm loaded down with baggage and nothing you could want to do to me is something I haven't done thanks to those dirty, hateful fuckers."

Without a second thought, I pulled him into my arms. Tucking his head under my chin, I ran a hand up and down his back. "Shhh, don't wanna hear shit like that. Me telling you no tonight has nothing to do with any of that."

"Then why? All this pain, all the shit they did to me. I

never got a say. Never got to tell them no"—his sad giggle was laced with pain—"well, I told them no, but that just got them off quicker." With his head buried in my chest, hot tears soaking my skin, Zane went on. "Always dreamed of falling in love. Finding someone who wanted me for me, not just the pain they wanted to dish out. But I don't know shit about love. Don't know a damned thing about being with someone who isn't paying for me and demanding I be high as a kite." A sob shuddered through him. "Fuck. I've never gotten off with another person because *I* wanted to do it. I know I can get hard..." He paused, biting his lip and looking up at me. "Happens all the time when I'm around you. But she used to force me to take what she laughingly called *your magic little pill* so the buyers would get all giddy thinking I was hard for them."

I held him tighter, hating every damn word that came out of his mouth, but determined to let him talk it out. No one should have that type of pain buried inside them.

"The women were the worst," he started. "No, that's not true. They were all monsters. The men hurt me the worst; being rough, not prepping me, slapping me around—fuck, maybe I would have liked that kind of sex with someone I loved and trusted, but now they've ruined me." He shook his head. "But I hated the women. Hilary would force the pill down my throat, wait for the effects to kick in—talk about a mind fuck when you don't want to be hard, yet your dick has no choice thanks to the chemicals—and then she'd let the buyer in. The women who paid for me..." He shuddered, lost in thought. "They always acted like I was hard for them. All the buyers, men and women, old and young, they'd get off on the fact I was hard and ejaculated. It's not like I *wanted* to come—" A sob wracked his lean frame.

"Shhhh, princess," I whispered, wanting to hold him close forever and absorb every single ounce of his pain. "That's a mind fuck and a half. What you went through was wrong, complete and total shit, and you didn't deserve any of it." I tipped his chin and nuzzled my nose against his—totally unfamiliar territory for me, but it felt right with Zane.

Any idea why damn near everything feels so right with him?

Clearing my throat and pushing away the thought, I pressed my forehead to his. "No more drugs. You come to me sober and you can control every single move we make. But I will *never* fuck around with someone who can't one-thousand-percent give consent. Mostly because of my fucked-up past, but also because it's just the right thing to do." I scoffed. "Not that me and *the right thing* are very well acquainted."

Zane shook his head. "You're wrong. You may have a past like the rest of us, but you're a good person."

I started to protest, but Zane cut me off.

"No, you *are* a good person. Have you made mistakes? Maybe. But were a lot of your decisions for the best to keep people from being hurt? I'm guessing, yes." Zane pressed a kiss to my chin. "Don't be so hard on yourself." He swayed a bit in my arms. "Sometime, maybe we can swap stories. I think it would do us good to get some of the shit out in the open..."

"But?"

He giggled. "But right now, I'm about to pass out."

I moved him toward his bed.

"Stay with me?" he asked, his words thick with sleep and drug.

Never in my life had I shared a bed with anyone for longer than it took to fuck them and leave.

And yet, here you are climbing into bed with your gorgeous princess. Ready to hold him through the night to ease his pain. Ready to give him what he's never had.

My nostrils flared at the errant thoughts.

Maybe even ready to hand over your heart.

Fuck that shit.

No.

I liked Zane. I'd spent over two months getting to know him—whether I'd wanted to or not, not that I was complaining. I had no issues with letting him use me for sex if it meant giving him some control and power back after the way Hilary abused him.

I'd kill each and every one of those dirty, fucking bastards who hurt him.

Raped him.

They raped a child.

Period.

I'd do anything I could to help him see them all pay.

I'd hold Hilary while the same pain was inflicted on her if that's what Zane wanted. I'd carve her heart out for him, let him watch her suffer and scream in agony as she died.

But I wouldn't give him my heart.

Not because I didn't want to.

But because I wasn't sure I had a heart to give.

Not sure I ever had.

Zane curled into my chest with a sigh as I pulled the blanket up over us.

As I watched his inky lashes flutter over porcelain skin, his blood-red lips parted in a sweet, soft snore, something gripped my chest and held tight.

If I *did* have a heart and the ability to love the way this man needed to be loved, I'd pour every bit of that love into Zane and hold on forever.

CHAPTER 8
ZANE

Stretching, moaning into the heated strength wrapped around me, I took a moment to luxuriate in waking in Holter's arms. Never had I slept so soundly and comfortably.

And then the night before slammed into me and I groaned in embarrassment.

"What's wrong?" Holter asked, his sleep-roughened words even gruffer than usual.

"Oh, nothing." I pressed my face into his chest, breathing deeply of last night's soap and everything that made this man. "Just dying."

"Are you sick? What did you take?" He quickly morphed into vigilante protector mode, reminding me that I'd never felt as close to someone—so safe in his presence—as I did to Holt.

I could have gone that route. Agreed it was the drugs. Allowed myself to avoid the difficult conversation. My past had forced me to push away the bad in order to survive and I could do that, there in Holt's arms, and he'd probably let me act as if nothing had happened.

At least for a short time.

But whatever had sparked between Holter and me from that very first day had taken root, sprouted leaves, and grown into something I'd never had with anyone else. It was a friendship, but more. Infatuation and attraction, but more. From the moment he'd let me live and brought me to The Woods, a pull deep in my gut had anchored me to this man and made me scoff a little less at the possibility of soul mates.

"It's not the drugs," I mumbled against his chest. Being curled into his big, warm body had a lot of unfamiliar and exciting feelings roaring through me. I knew I was fucked up in the sex, arousal, and intimacy department, but, for the first time since Hilary sold me, I felt safe, secure, and free to explore.

Whether that was because of the therapy I'd been working my way through or because of the quick and easy bond between Holter and me.

Probably a combination of the two.

"You wanna talk about it? Or save it for therapy?"

"Neither? Both?" I groaned. "What time is it?"

"We've got hours before we need to leave. Brunch and chat?"

"You don't seem like the type of guy to do breakfast in bed and while away your time chatting with a fucked-up kid."

Holt gripped my chin gently and lifted my face to meet my eyes. "I'm not. Usually. Then I found this pretty princess and he messed me up. Has me doing shit I just don't do." He paused, breathing in deeply and closing his eyes as if savoring the mixed scent of our sleep-warm bodies. "And you're *not* fucked up."

"I am—"

"You lived through some beyond-fucked-up shit, but deep in your core, you're still the amazing, beautiful, kind-hearted Zane you were born to be."

"If I'm so kind-hearted, why do I want to hurt them all so bad?" Raw pain laced my words.

"Because you're human." Holt pressed a kiss to the top of my head. "Go shower. I'll make food. If you want to talk, we can."

He rolled from the bed and stretched.

Shifting to my knees, I reached out and wrapped an arm around his waist. "Wait."

"What's up, princess?" Holter turned to face me, my position kneeling on the mattress putting me face-to-face with him.

"Thank you," I whispered. I kissed him, bringing our lips together in a soft, warm mating. For a fraction of a second, I worried he wasn't going to kiss me back. But then Holt's big hand cupped the back of my head, his fingers carding through my hair.

As his tongue slid against mine, heating my body with a desire I feared I'd never experience, my soft whimper filled the air.

When Holt broke the kiss, he held onto the sides of my head, his forehead pressed against mine. "What was that for?"

"Just grateful you didn't kill me."

He closed his eyes and breathed in deep. "You don't

owe me anything for that. Don't ever think you owe me *anything*."

I bit my lip. "Kinda just wanted to do it too."

He smirked, his eyes still closed. "Not gonna argue with that one." He ran his big hand up and down my back, nuzzling his nose against my ear. "Go shower. You want coffee or tea?"

"Tea, please."

By the time I'd exited the shower, the apartment smelled of food. I heard Holt talking to some of the other guys and I thought about joining them. I liked all the guys I lived with. They were good people, fun to be around, and they'd taken me in without question. But I was still wallowing a bit in last night's embarrassment and didn't really feel like socializing.

When Holt returned to the room with a tray, my heart flip-flopped.

"Lorien suggested a tray rather than trying to carry it all." A sheepish blush painted his cheeks. "Would you rather eat in the kitchen?"

I shook my head and patted the mattress. I'd only known Holter for a couple months, but he'd become my protector, my friend, a confidant, and someone I enjoyed spending time with. I'd watched him morph slowly from a detached loner to someone who thrived on friendships he would have sworn he didn't need. Whether he liked it or not—or wanted to admit it—belonging and having people care about him hit him deep.

In my wildest dreams, I'd hoped to find a man who would be patient with me and support me through the healing I needed to do.

Then, I'd found Holter.

The hunter.

The hitman.

The dark loner.

And he was so much more than I'd ever hoped for, if only he'd realize how much he had to give.

We sipped our tea.

I devoured an apple Holter had kindly cut into pieces for me.

He took bites of a croissant.

The silence surrounding us brought me peace. Nowhere to be, no expectations, no one wanting to hurt me.

Just me and Holt.

And the stunt I pulled the night before.

I groaned.

"What?" Holter shot me a concerned look.

"I'm really sorry about last night."

"You wanna talk about any of it?"

I shrugged, my thoughts taking me back to the nightmare I lived through. "I hated the drugs. Swore I'd never use them again. She forced them on me." Picking at a loose thread on the blanket, my cheeks heated. "And then the first time I decide to flirt, I can't even find the courage to do it without chemicals. I won't ever touch the vasodilators again, but I thought something to loosen me up, kinda a shot of confidence, would help. I'm sorry."

"There's nothing to apologize for."

"You seemed angry."

"I wasn't angry at you, just at the situation. Consent

under the influence isn't consent." His finger grazed my leg. "I was interested. *Am* interested. But it's a line I just won't cross."

"God," I moaned, my face in my hands. "I luck out by surviving a hitman, land in the most perfect place to live with people I couldn't have even dreamed of having as friends, find a job, and get the sexiest, most caring roommate in the world..." My emotions escaped in a growl. "And then I go and mess everything up."

"You didn't mess anything up." Holt's warm hand on my bare thigh sent heat through me. He cleared his throat. "I haven't told anyone about my past. Suffice it to say that I watched my mom used and abused more than once because she was under the influence of whatever shit her boyfriend of the moment convinced her or forced her to take." He shook his head. "Even after she kicked me out, I swore I'd *never* take advantage of anyone who wasn't one hundred percent sober."

"Why'd she kick you out?"

His swallow was audible and he stared, lost in memories. For a moment, I thought he wasn't going to answer me, but he finally cleared his throat again and spoke. "One of her boyfriends got super rough. I was about sixteen and I couldn't take it anymore—I'd watched it for too many years. I was big and already pretty intimidating—didn't have friends at school; who wants to be friends with the new kid, the kid whose mom is the new junkie whore in town?" He huffed out a breath. "Anyway, this asshole got rough and I stepped between them. He went ballistic and attacked me. I fought back. Once I started punching him, I couldn't stop

—like sixteen years of hurt and fear and rage came pouring out of me. When my mom realized what I'd done, she freaked out." He paused, running a hand over his eyes. "Back then, I thought she was mad I'd killed her boyfriend, her supplier—thought she picked him over me. Knowing what I know now, I think she probably panicked that I'd get taken away from her and end up in the system—she'd been in foster care and it really fucked her up. She was always hyper-vigilant about keeping me out of the system. So, when she realized he was dead, she screamed at me to leave. Told me to get out, get far away, and never come back." He paused, lost in thought. "Always wondered what she did with the body. There was no way she could have inflicted the type of damage I did, so I have no clue how she explained it or how she got rid of him. Hell, maybe she left town at the same time I did." His head thumped against the wall. "All I knew back then was I was sixteen, I'd just killed a man, and my mom—who I loved despite how fucked up our life was because of her—had thrown me out."

My heart hurt for him. "Where did you go?"

"Here and there. Kinda like now. This is the longest I've stayed put since I was sixteen. I looked older, so most people didn't question me being on my own. I did a lot of things I'm not proud of, but I kept myself alive."

"You're not a bad person, Holt," I whispered. "If I have to believe it about me, you have to believe it about you."

His head lolled to the side to look at me. "Easier said than done. I've done shit. Bad shit."

"But you've also done good shit. I know you have.

Don't ask me how I know, I just do. The way you took me in, saved me from Hilary, are still protecting me." I shifted to face him. "Do you know what happened to your mom? Or even want to know?"

He shook his head. "I can't imagine she's still alive. That was well over ten years ago. She wasn't in great physical or mental health. I think I mostly think of her as dead. At first, it was because I was hurt and angry. Now, it's just because I can't realistically picture her still living the way she did. I think I'd rather imagine her peacefully dead than traumatically living—if that makes any sense."

"It makes all the sense in the world," I whispered. "I've had those exact same thoughts ever since the first buyer stepped into my room."

Holt tensed beside me.

I covered his hand with mine. "Some days, the only thing that kept me going was knowing she'd move to the children if I was gone. I overheard her talking to one of the buyers once. He was one of the meanest—old and rich, got off harder the more I hurt. Anyway, he told her, 'You better never let this one go. My money is yours as long as you keep his sweet little ass ready for me. The offer still stands. I'll buy him outright for whatever he'd bring in for you in one year.'" I shivered. "Hilary laughed in his face and said no way. Then he mentioned the children's home as a buffet. She told him if and when her little Zaney wasn't available, she'd pick the finest from the home just for her buyers."

The words flowed out and drained me, but telling someone the hateful truth always helped. Especially when they believed me and didn't treat me like I was the one to blame.

I took a deep breath, aware Holt was tense beside me. Cupping his jaw, I nuzzled my nose against his. "Thank you for telling me your story. As someone who has never once been given the chance to consent, I understand your take on substances."

"Thank you for understanding and for trusting me with your story," Holt said, his words gruff like he was chewing nails. "Each time you offer a little bit of your pain, I want to kill her even more. And not just kill her, hurt her the way she hurt you."

"Yeah, I get it. It's a mind fuck."

We sat quietly for a moment, finishing our food and tea.

When Holt finished placing the tray on the floor, I took his hand. "This is probably all gonna be a jumbled mess, but I'm gonna try to get it out in some semblance of making sense. I want to be wanted for *me* by someone who isn't a fucked up perv. Wanted because someone cares for me, not because my body is available for purchase." I scowled, feeling as if my words weren't making sense in the least. "I want to *want* someone—until you, I always wondered if I'd ever be able to find that attraction and desire. I want sex even though sex is part of my baggage. But I want it on my terms with someone I trust. There are a few things I'm not sure I'll ever be able to do, too many bad memories. And I don't think I can do anything rough—at least not for now."

Holt squeezed my hand and just let me talk.

"I know I'm fucked up and I know the amount of

understanding and patience I need is probably the biggest turn off—"

Holter grunted and gripped my chin. "Nothing about you is a turn off. Anything you need, say the word. As slow as you need, every step of the way." He ran a thumb over my lips. "I'm not the relationship type, but I can be what you need for the time being."

My heart stuttered, teetering on the edge of falling over the cliff. "And what if I want more?"

Holter shook his head. "That's not something I can promise, but we have right now."

"And down the road?"

He winced. "Talk of the future isn't a thing for me. I never know where I'll be. But I can give you this part of me for now, if you want it."

Selfishly, I wanted more. Wanted to start something with the man I used to only dream about and see where it could go. It was dangerous to get involved with a man I already wanted to hand my heart to. Knowing Holt had no intention of returning my feelings meant heartache down the line.

But the draw to this man was too strong. I'd lived through the worst kind of hell; I could survive a bit of heartbreak.

"What can we do?"

"We'll start slow. But you need to tell me up front what things you don't want to try, things you know are a hard-no."

I nodded. "Kissing is good. There were a few who liked to kiss and they made me want to barf, but your kisses aren't like that."

Holt stroked a thumb down my chin. "Good. What else?"

"Don't call me *little boy*. Don't talk about how hard I am for you—it used to be just the Viagra, and now it would be for real, but those words are in my nightmares." I swallowed thickly. "I want to suck you off, but I need it to be at my speed. Not too hard or deep. You can suck me off, just again don't talk about how hard I am, and *please* don't make me call you Daddy." A shiver shook through my body and Holt's body nearly shimmered with rage. "Actual penetrative sex needs lots of prep. Has to be slow and gentle in the beginning at least."

Holt wrapped an arm around my shoulders and pulled me close, pressing a kiss to the top of my head. "I'm so fucking sorry, Zane." His words like gravel. "You are gorgeous and good and so fucking special; you didn't deserve any of that. Fuck, no one deserves that."

A sob wracked my shoulders. "I'm so fucked up. I'm sorry."

He lifted my chin, feathering a kiss over my forehead, the tip of my nose, and finally landing just below my bottom lip. "I will say this a million times if you need me to, and I'll repeat it a million more until you believe it. You aren't fucked up. You're you. You're good, you're beautiful, you're worthy." Wiping my tears with his thumb, he pressed our foreheads together. "I want to give you what you've never had; want to make it good for you, but you have to tell me if I screw up."

I nodded.

"No, Zane. I'm serious. *Any time*; doesn't matter if it

wasn't on your list. Doesn't matter if you liked it last time and this time you don't. You have to tell me." Holter drew in a deep breath. "I must be insane letting myself get involved in any kind of way"—he narrowed his eyes and shook his head—"and not because of your trauma, just because I don't do the whole *involved* thing." He let out a grumbly noise. "But I can't stop wanting you."

"You want me?" I whispered.

Holter chuckled. "Can't stop. Wanting to kiss you and hold you. Want to take you so high and watch you break into all the pretty, colorful pieces."

I cuddled close.

"But I can't stand the thought of hurting you."

"You won't."

"I've hurt people, Zane."

I shook my head. "You've hurt bad people, people who deserved it. Do I deserve to be hurt?"

"Of course not."

"I trust you." Placing my hand over his heart, I went on. "I trust you more than anyone since my parents. You won't hurt me."

"I can't be the happily ever after you dreamed about." A rawness laced his words.

Couldn't? Or *wouldn't*? Or maybe it was just that he didn't realize how much love he had in that dark heart of his.

"How do you know that? Have you ever been in love?" I asked.

Holter snorted. "Love isn't for me."

"Would you accept it if it came along?"

He narrowed his eyes, a smirk teasing his lips. "You're a determined little thing, aren't you?"

I shrugged. "You see the best in me. I see the best in you; you're too stubborn to see it. I'm just saying, if love came into your life, would you let it live there? Give it your heart?"

He shook his head and chuckled. "My fair princess is a dreamer through and through."

"When your life is one big nightmare, it helps to have dreams to get you through."

Holt sobered at that, a thumb tracing along my lips. "I'm glad you could dream, princess." Then he dipped his head and caught my mouth. Soft and sweet morphed into silky heat, a whimper escaping my lips.

I wasn't fooled. Distracting kisses didn't cover up the fact Holter hadn't answered the question, but for the time being, I had other things to occupy me.

Holter yanked me on top of him, our chests pressed together, our hard cocks nestled next to each other with a perfect friction. The kiss went on and on, my blood sizzling with an unfamiliar, delicious desire just under the surface, but we had all the time in the world.

No hurry.

No pain.

No nightmare.

Just Holt and me.

Pausing, I pressed my forehead to his, our chests flush together, and just breathed him in. Savored the moment; his scent, the beating of our hearts, the warmth of his gentle hands. Hands that had killed, but hands that brought me nothing but protection and pleasure.

"It's your show, princess," he murmured against my lips. "What do you want to do?"

I rubbed myself against him and moaned. "Wanna get off, but don't want it over too fast."

Holter chuckled. "Is jerking off something you like to do?"

Biting my lip, I nodded. "Used to do it...before." My cheeks were on fire. "But I want you to touch me."

Holt's hands slid from my back to my ass, pulling me close and grinding our hips together. "First, I *am* touching you." He pressed a kiss to my nose. Where did this man get the idea he wasn't capable of intimate relationships? "Second, we have time. Maybe not forever, but we don't have to get straight to it right away."

I snorted. "Straight."

He smiled and rolled his eyes. "You know what I mean. We can take our time, go slowly."

"You'll jerk off with me?" I asked, my mouth suddenly dry at the thought of Holter spread out on my bed as he watched me and stroked himself off.

"If that's what you want." Holter's fiery eyes caught mine, our hips continuing to roll together.

"I *want*—"

He shut me up with a kiss. When we finally broke apart, both of us panting, he nipped at my bottom lip. "Slow, princess. We'll get to it." He smacked my ass lightly and rubbed the spot. "Now, get naked so we can get off."

CHAPTER 9

HOLTER

If I didn't keep myself focused, I was going to bust a nut within about thirty seconds. I was in way over my head, but there was nowhere else I wanted to be.

Zane and I leaned against the headboard, hard, leaking cocks in hand, and stroked ourselves. His eyes traveled from my hand to my face and back again, tongue darting out to wet his lips, teeth catching the plump, red flesh.

This was Zane's show and I was just along for the ride.

But if I didn't keep myself in check, I'd blow it.

Literally.

"Tell me what you're thinking," I demanded, forcing my fist to go slow and gentle on my dick. There was no hurry. Watching Zane was the real pleasure in this whole situation.

His eyes flew to mine and his nostrils flared.

"You don't have to," I said. "You're in control."

Zane shook his head. "I want to. Just haven't done this in a while." His cheeks pinked. "And never told anyone what I'm thinking."

Treading lightly, scared to death to say the wrong thing or bring a bad memory to mind, I watched him. Eyes never leaving his, my balls heavy between my legs, I thumbed over my slit. "You thinking about me?"

Zane whimpered and nodded.

"Tell me."

He bit his bottom lip and stroked faster. "Your mouth on me." The words left him in a rush. And then the flood gates opened. "Sucking me, licking my hole. Fingers opening me up." His breath caught and he eyed my cock hungrily. "Inside me. God, Holt, I want you inside me. Want you to make it so good."

His words went straight to my balls and pre-cum leaked from my cock. "Mmmm," I hummed. "You'll make such pretty noises when I tongue fuck your little hole."

Zane whimpered and jerked himself faster, his head falling back, the slim lines of his body arched and corded. "Please," he begged.

"You'll be so tight on my fingers. So tight on my cock when I slide inside."

"Fuck," Zane gasped. "Oh, fuck. I'm gonna come."

"Come here," I growled. "Between my legs. Come on me."

Zane's eyes flew open wide and he scrambled between my spread legs. Kneeling, leaking cock in hand, he jerked himself. "Wanna suck you."

"Not yet," I said. "Can I touch you?"

"Yessss," he moaned.

I sat up straight, my dick and balls screaming in protest, and took his slim hips between my hands. Bending, I licked over his slit before taking him between my lips as I moved a hand to caress his balls.

Zane jerked his hips, groaning as his orgasm flooded my mouth. The flavor of him on my tongue ruined me for any other man and I knew I'd dream of his cum.

Instead of savoring his load, I popped off and leaned backwards, pulling him with me until his still-pulsing cock was pressed against mine. "Your show, princess. Get me off."

Zane whimpered through a smile, his hooded eyes trailing down our bodies as his hips began to thrust. "Talk to me," he demanded.

Running my hands up and down his back, getting my palms full of his plump ass cheeks, I murmured at his ear, "Your cum tastes amazing. Next time, I'm gonna work you open with my fingers while I suck that gorgeous cock. I'll play with your prostate until you shoot your load on my tongue."

His lips were on mine in a flash. Tongue stroking and lips clinging, he devoured my mouth as we frotted together. "Fuck, Holt," he moaned. "I wanna feel you in my ass so bad. Wanna make it good and forget the bad."

With the image of Zane spread open for me, taking my cock, my body tensed and I shot long, hot ropes of cum between us. Rolling Zane to the mattress, I moved to my side and wrapped him in my arms, pulling him close to my chest. Pressing a kiss to his temple, I had a brief moment of panic.

That was too much.

Too soon.

He wasn't ready.

"That was amazing," Zane whispered against my chest.

"Yeah?"

"Mmhm..."

We drifted off into a sex-induced sleep.

When we woke sometime later, Zane moaned. "As much as I'd love to stay in bed and go for round two, I have a drag debut I don't want to miss."

"My dick can't compete with that," I teased, slapping a hand on his plump ass.

"Your dick is an award-winner for sure." He pushed up on his elbow and cupped my face in his hand. "That was the first positive sex experience I've ever had. I don't know why I trust you so easily and feel so right with you. And I don't want you with me just because you feel obligated, but if you're willing, I'd love to keep replacing the bad with the good."

"Being with you isn't an obligation." I pressed a kiss to his lips.

I was in dangerous, unchartered territory with Zane, but stopping wasn't an option. I was in too deep already.

Too attached.

Too involved.

And man enough to admit, way too smitten.

"I can't make promises for the future, but for the present, I can be here every damn day if it means pushing away the bad and bringing in the good."

Zane's eyes filled with tears and his face melted into

the most gorgeous smile. "That sounds absolutely amazing."

We showered together and got dressed. Zane looked amazing in his disguise as he grabbed two apples and headed out the door.

When he glanced over his shoulder, chewing on a big bite of apple, and grinned my way, I chuckled and rolled my eyes.

I was in so much fucking trouble.

Zane's drag persona was Mira-Mira and she was fucking hot as hell. The night of her debut, she absolutely owned the stage. The first night she performed, she brought down the house, but Mira-Mira was now consistently bringing in double and triple the crowd sizes that 7 had ever experienced.

Aiden and Felix hadn't done it just yet, but they'd been toying with the idea of having to split the crowd and do tickets as a first-come-first-served situation for the nights Mira-Mira performed.

It was a good problem to have and Zane was absolutely floating on Cloud Nine with how well his performance had been received.

"I *love* being Mira-Mira," he gushed one night a couple weeks after he debuted the show. I stood at his door during his bedtime routine. "She's fierce and in control. No one messes with her. She's brave."

Walking to stand behind him, I wrapped my arms around his waist and pressed a kiss to his neck. "She is.

She's fucking fearless and gorgeous and so damn talented." My words caught in my throat and I cleared whatever *that* was away. "But so are you. Don't forget where she came from," I whispered, placing my hand over his heart. "*You* are all of those things too. And I'm so fucking proud of you."

I'd never felt these feelings. Being proud of someone was new for me. I'd never had friends or family to *be* proud of. Zane owned me and my entire body quivered with the knowledge I'd fight to protect him to the death.

Watching him take to the stage and overcome even just a bit of his past had done something weird inside my chest. The first night I'd watched him, I'd seriously wondered if I was having a heart attack.

Zane nuzzled his nose to the underside of my jaw. "Sometimes, it's just easier to be those things when I'm her. I know I've been through a lot and overcome a lot—and I may never be *done* overcoming everything Hilary did to me—but being in my makeup and outfits just makes it easier to play the part of being strong and courageous sometimes."

"I get it..." I paused with a frown. "Well, maybe I don't *get it*, but that makes sense." I traced a finger down his cheek. "Your outfits *are* amazing—I probably hear twenty people a night gushing over your songs, the dance moves, and the outfits. And obviously, the makeup is fabulous."

"Obviously," Zane quipped.

Mira-Mira's performance included three songs mixed together. The overall mood of the show was dark and powerful which fit perfectly with who Zane was and what he'd survived.

Zane had worked hard to put together his song set for Mira-Mira's show. How he'd so perfectly mixed the songs was beyond me, but he used parts of "You Belong to Me" by Cat Pierce, "Start a War" by Klergy and Valerie Broussard, and "Castle" by Halsey.

He had the pearl stage, but he'd worked with the lighting tech to give the pearlescent décor a black tint and overall darkness. From the moment Mira-Mira walked onto the stage, she owned the place and had the audience eating from her hand, hanging on her every move.

Her outfit started more like a ballgown when she first came onto the stage. A blue bustier that hugged her torso until right above her belly button, blue poofy sleeves, a tiny yellow panty, and a red and yellow bustle-like, floor-length, open-in-the-front skirt, and red patent-leather boots. About a third of the way into the show, she stripped out of the skirt and the poofy sleeves, leaving her lean, lithe body in just the bustier, panties, and boots.

Her makeup was all dark and smoky, blood-red lips, and ridiculous lashes. Adding the jet-black, ass-length wig as the final touch had the crowd drooling and panting over Mira-Mira from the very first note of her song set until the last death-drop right before she crawled seductively to the front of the stage, whipped her hair 'round and 'round, and blew a kiss to the crowd.

"Speaking of feeling powerful," Zane hedged, his big

brown eyes meeting mine in the mirror. "Can we try again?"

Sex between us had been going well. Slow and simple, but it was good.

Damn, it was good.

We'd kept things to watching each other touch ourselves, jerking each other off, and me sucking Zane off. We both wanted more, but going slow had been necessary.

There had been a couple set-backs when a certain word, scent, image, or sound took Zane back to the trauma and we needed to take a break. Thanks to Zane's never-ending optimism and determination to take back what Hilary and her buyers had stolen from him—and his unwavering commitment to working through his trauma in therapy—he'd learned quickly the importance of communication. He was quick to tell me if something wasn't working and very open when it came to talking about what he was feeling.

Being with Zane had taught me a lot as well. I'd never been a talker. Not one for feelings or shit like that. But Zane had opened me up from the beginning and everything we did together—everything we talked about—had me wanting to pour my damn heart into him. The kid had changed me from the moment I laid eyes on him and I couldn't even bother to be upset about it because he had me under some kind of spell.

"We can do anything you want. Just stop me if it's wrong." It was hard sometimes, worrying I'd say or do something to take Zane back to that nightmare. But communicating—knowing he'd stop me if something wasn't right—knowing the triggers to avoid was helpful. And Zane knew I'd never purposely hurt him. There were times when a word or something similar made him freeze and we'd talk it through later to figure out it wasn't even something he'd known was a trigger.

Zane stood and slipped his big, flowy t-shirt over his head. Naked, his pale skin slightly pink from an earlier shower, his long, slim cock already hard for me, he turned off the bathroom light and pressed his hands against my chest. Exploring my chest, tweaking my nipples, he smiled at my grunt of pleasure. Trailing his hands up to my shoulders, he wrapped his arms around my neck. Warmth pressed between us, my body sighing as if soaking in everything he had to give me.

Pushing me backwards until my legs met the bed, Zane smiled up at me. "You're so good to me," he whispered, going up on tiptoes to capture my mouth. "I love how patient you are with me. How gentle. How you let me take control. You make me feel so powerful, so cherished..." Those big, brown eyes looked up at me from beneath thick, black lashes. "So loved."

He wasn't wrong. I *did* love him. I wasn't sure when it had happened—some parts of me felt as if I'd loved Zane my entire life...or like my life hadn't really even started until that moment in the alley.

I wasn't ready to admit it, but I loved him. In my own way—which was likely fucked up and sure to lead to heartache.

But I loved him.

Instead of words, I kissed him, hoping it would be enough for now.

For now? Isn't that all you've got? Aren't you still planning to leave?

The thought took my breath away.

Leaving was still at the back of my mind, but it felt less and less like the right thing to do every day.

Could I stay? Could I make a life in Fairwood?

Or would I be better off to see Zane through until Hilary and his other abusers were punished and then leave? Let him build a life for himself here without me standing in his way.

He deserved a fresh start with someone who could give him a future.

Why can't that someone be you?

"Holt?" Zane asked, concern etched on his delicate features as he pulled away from the kiss. "You okay? Where'd you go?"

Pulling myself from the thoughts, I brought myself back to the bedroom, back to Zane. "I'm here, princess."

Always here.

With Zane.

And this crazy stupid thing we'd started.

Zane smiled and bit his lip. "Wanna suck you, but don't wanna get off that way." He bent, his tongue playing over a nipple.

We'd tried him blowing me a couple times, but he'd needed to stop. "You don't have to—"

"I *want* to. Want *your* taste on my tongue, the heavy weight of *your* cock between my lips." His breath caught as he paused. "*Your* scent in my nose when I think of doing that. But I think just sucking you then moving to us both getting off another way might be the best plan for now."

I cupped his face and pressed a kiss to his forehead, so in awe of this beautiful, strong, determined man. Helping replace all the bad memories with good was a responsibility I would honor and cherish forever. "Your show. I'm with you every step of the way."

Zane nodded and dropped to his knees, his nose nuzzling against my boxers. Slipping his thumbs into my waistband, he looked up at me. "This okay?"

My sweet, sweet princess never once failed to make sure *I* was comfortable with what we were doing. Always wanting to be sure we were both on board. So much had been taken from him and forced onto him, yet his heart beat so good and true in his genuine concern for others.

Brushing his cheek with the back of my hand, I whispered, "It's okay. Stop when you need to." Emotion roughened my words. What Zane trusted me with—what he *gave* me—sometimes it was too much. Too much for my head to take in, too much for my heart to believe. How could this beautiful man—inside and out—trust *me* with something as sacred as the rebuilding of his body and soul?

Cool air hit my skin as the boxers made their way to the floor. Leaning back, my weight on my arms to keep myself from touching his head, I fought the urge to close my eyes and just melt into his exploration. But I couldn't pull my gaze from him. The way he breathed me in deep, his nose pressed into the trimmed thatch of hair at the base of my cock. He roamed lower, his tongue and nose becoming well-acquainted with my balls. When his sweet little tongue flicked through the pre-cum leaking from my slit, I groaned. And then my actual life left my body when Zane spread his lips around my cock and sucked me deep.

Every.

Damn.

Time.

Every single touch from Zane always short-circuited my synapses.

We'd learned from past experiences that I couldn't touch his head during a blow job, and he couldn't take me all the way to the back of his throat, but he used his mouth and fist to stroke me—his other hand playing with my balls—and had me close to exploding within seconds.

"Zane," I grunted. "Too good. Don't wanna come this way." That wasn't exactly true. I would have gladly unloaded down his throat, but I knew it wasn't what he wanted.

He scrambled up my body, pushing me to the mattress, his sticky lips finding mine. He tasted uniquely of Zane and my pre-cum, and I loved it; wanted to devour his mouth. Wanted him to taste of me forever.

"What do you want?" I panted against his lips.

"Suck me and finger me."

As if I'd ever say no to those pretty, pleading words.

I wrapped him in my arms, holding him close, just breathing him in and savoring the way our bodies melted together, how we fit like the perfect puzzle pieces. "Get comfortable, however you want."

Zane paused and gave my words some thought.

While he rolled from my chest and positioned himself on the mattress, I grabbed the lube from the bedside drawer. We'd purposely not stocked up on condoms.

For multiple reasons.

One, Zane had insisted we both get tested. We'd both had negative tests before we met, but he wanted a fresh start for whatever this thing was between us.

"Hilary insisted on negative tests from her buyers," Zane had told me once. "Always fucked with my head that she'd sell my body to whoever was willing to pay, but she wanted to protect me from any infections." He shook his head. "I know it was more to keep her buyers happy—she lost a *lot* of money during the two weeks I was out due to needing to be on a strong round of antibiotics." His eyes had taken on that faraway look. "Pretty shitty when an STI is a welcome break from your own personal hell. Anyway, *that* particular buyer was banned and Hilary upped the testing protocol even more after that."

Another reason we didn't have condoms was because I stupidly thought lack of condoms would quell my burning desire to slide into Zane's tight hole. I wasn't going to do it—not without his consent and both of us feeling like we were ready—but not having condoms definitely didn't temper that longing.

And Zane had blushed, biting his lip when he told me, "If we ever get to a time when it feels right, I want to take you without anything between us. Hilary insisted on condoms. Another mind-fuck..." he'd paused, his lips twisted into a pained sneer, "because I'm *grateful* she required it, but how the fuck can I be grateful she made my *rapists* wear condoms?" He'd held his head in his hands and cried that day. All I could do was hold him as he let it out.

And seethe with rage as I imagined all the ways I wanted to kill each and every person who'd ever hurt him.

So, we'd decided no condoms if and when we ever reached that point.

But I'd bought lube.

Zane was on his side, top leg bent and resting against the mattress. The position allowed for a gorgeous view of his ass and balls, his hard dick partly hidden and smearing pre-cum on the blanket.

Skimming my hand over the smooth skin of his ass, I leaned in and pressed a kiss to the plump flesh. "Can I rim you?"

Zane whimpered and rocked his hips. "Fuck, Holt. Fuck."

I waited as he ground his dick into the mattress, his pretty little hole clenching with what I hoped was anticipation. "Yes or no?"

"Yes," he gasped. "Fuck, yes."

Burying my face between his cheeks, I pressed a kiss to his pucker, smiling against his sensitive flesh when he cried out. The guys would hear if they were home, but I didn't care. They all knew Zane and I had something going on and I wasn't about to tell Zane he had to hide his pleasure.

He'd told me once how terrifying it was that his cries for help, his screams of pain, went ignored. I'd vowed that day to never silence him—pain or pleasure, facts or opinions, serious or silly, I'd *never* make him think he wasn't being heard.

Circling his rim with my tongue, I worked him until he was soft and wet. Shifting so my face was dick-level, I draped his top leg over my shoulder. Pumping lube onto my fingers, I slicked them over his hole as I took his dick between my lips.

The bitter, salty tang of Zane's pre-cum coated my tongue and I sucked greedily. His tight balls pressed against my chin as he thrust his cock deep. I knew the frantic, whimpery noises escaping Zane meant he wasn't far from orgasm. Pressing my finger against his hole, I popped off his shaft long enough to ask, "You okay? This good?"

Zane groaned a yes and I swallowed him back down as my finger breached his tight ring. He gripped my hair, his warm thigh pressed tightly against my cheek and ear, and begged for another finger. "Please, Holt. Oh god, please. I want more."

I loved that he found pleasure in what we were doing. Nothing in my life would ever be as fulfilling as making this man feel good. Knowing even the slightest bit about his past meant my entire being was focused on nothing but bringing him pleasure, making him feel loved and cherished. I would spend the rest of my life helping him replace all of the negative, painful nightmares of his past with new, positive experiences.

The rest of your life, huh? Doesn't sound like someone who's leaving at the end of nine months.

I pushed away the thought. Now wasn't the time to

psychoanalyze myself or whatever Zane and I had going on.

Slipping a second finger into him, the tight squeeze of his muscles gripping my fingers. I used my thumb to caress his perineum as my tongue swirled around his throbbing cock.

Curling my fingers, I searched for that spot deep within.

The keening moan and hard rocking of Zane's hips told me I'd found what I was looking for seconds before his release exploded in my mouth, coating my tongue, his warmth sliding down my throat.

"Oh fuck, oh fuck, oh fuck," Zane chanted as he fisted my hair and poured himself into me, his ass clenching around my fingers.

When he'd caught his breath, Zane rolled his hips. "Your turn," he said, his words still thick with desire. He groaned in protest when I pulled my fingers from his body, but shifted our position until I was on my back. Straddling my waist, Zane moved so his ass crack encased my cock and began to rock his hips, his undulations giving just the right friction to my throbbing dick.

The spit and lube I'd used to finger his ass now coated my shaft as he rode me. I grunted, fighting the urge to shift just slightly and slide into his tight body. I wanted him so fucking badly. Wanted to own each and every part of him, wanted our bodies to be one. But I gripped his hips and let him jack me off with his pretty, plump ass.

"Gonna have you inside me." He pressed his hands to

my chest and slid his crack up and down my shaft. "Feel so good. Just for you. Stretch me open and give me your cum."

"Fuuuuck," I growled, Zane's words going straight to my balls. I exploded, my hot load coating his crack, his balls, and my cock as he continued to ride me.

Zane cried out, his own cock dribbling another attempt at an orgasm before he collapsed onto my chest. Pressing kisses to my jaw, Zane sighed. "Fuck, we get better and better at that every damn time. It's so fucking good." He took a shaky breath. "Thank you, Holt."

"You don't owe me thanks," I started.

"I know I don't *owe* you, but I'm grateful anyway. What we have, what you give me, it's so good. You help erase my demons with every kiss and touch."

I held him close, my lips against his temple as we both basked in our post-orgasm bliss. How could I walk away from this? My heart clenched, already filled with pain and dread over leaving Zane.

But staying wasn't an option. *Staying* had never been an option. Not when I killed my mom's boyfriend. Not when I'd brought in, harmed, and sometimes killed people in town after town.

And not here in Fairwood.

Why not? You have a permanent place—well, as permanent as you've ever had—with actual friends, a steady job, and a man you've fallen in love with.

The thought scared me, if I was being honest.

Moving on was what I did.

It was what I knew best.

No roots, no one knowing my business, no one counting on me.

But the constant moving was exhausting. I could admit that much to myself.

Despite my head thumping *you need to leave* over and over, my heart clung to Zane. "Why not?" my heart's rhythm seemed to ask with each beat. "Why not stay?"

Why not, indeed.

CHAPTER 10
ZANE

I couldn't help the proud feeling nearly bursting from my chest. The crowds at 7 on the nights of my performances were absolutely huge. I'd known working behind the bar had earned us some new regulars, but Mira-Mira had been a huge hit and brought in money like nobody's business.

Mira-Mira was a queen—powerful, courageous, and ready to eat you up and spit you out. She was *me*. The me who wasn't broken. She wasn't scared. She didn't stand for shit—Mira-Mira would *never* let herself be used.

Bitch, please. You know damn well you stayed to save those kids. Mira-Mira's voice was always loud in my head. *And don't start this shit about me being stronger than you. I* am *you. Push all that shit from your pretty little head. You were the victim. You stayed for the kids—you stayed for whatever reason you stayed, you don't owe anyone a damn explanation. You are a powerful and courageous queen, ready to bring down every damn person who ever hurt you.*

My brown eyes, highlighted with heavy, smoky

makeup, stared back at me from the mirror as I untucked after my performance.

7 had become my home, just as The Woods and the guys had become my home. I'd likely not be doing death drops for the rest of my life—I'd hang up my new form of therapy and release through drag at *some* point—but, beyond my love of the power and courage drag allowed me—I knew Fairwood was where I belonged. I'd been born here and my family name was all over the town. Hilary tried to destroy me, but I was patiently coming after her and she'd pay for what she'd done.

Holt had connections who'd put us in touch with certain members of the Fairwood law enforcement, as well as some state organizations, who were helping us build up a case against Hilary and her buyers.

He'd also worked with the police and other agencies to get eyes on the inside of the children's home in order to protect the kids while the investigation went on.

Between the guys at The Woods, Holter, the connections of his connections, and the departments who were actually taking my story seriously, we were slowly—very slowly—gathering information, tracking down buyers, monitoring them, and bringing in enough shit against them to bring them down.

Hilary, too.

She was the easiest because she truly thought she was invincible and took absolutely zero precautions. Most of her buyers at least *tried* to fly under the radar and keep their predatory behavior on the down low. However, the richer and more powerful the buyers, the less likely they were to keep things discreet.

I spent several hours with the sex crimes units from both the town of Fairwood and the state. The questions were grueling, but I had my therapist and Holt to turn to after each interview. My notes had proved to be invaluable in hunting down the buyers. Once names and accusations were known, it was easy for the sex crimes investigators to dig deep. Those deep digs uncovered a shit ton—so much more than just what they were paying to do to me—and the crimes they'd eventually be charged with were set to be the biggest sex crime scandal in Fairwood, the state, and possibly even the country.

But the whole thing moved at a snail's pace.

I understood why. The more dirt they could gather on Hilary and the buyers, the better. And my stories and notes were good, but if the investigators could have *more* against them, more charges could be brought. The more proof of their disgusting crimes against children and adults, the better chance they'd spend the rest of their lives in prison.

Or worse.

My hope was for *worse.*

God, how I wanted revenge against them all.

Hilary the most.

She took my father away. She took away my childhood. She stole my innocence and hurt me physically, mentally, and emotionally in ways that many wouldn't have survived.

I survived.

I escaped.

And I was going to see them pay.

Every single one of them.

They'd lose everything.

They'd suffer.

And I'd thrive just to spite them.

Hilary tried to break me, tried to get rid of me, wanted me to suffer and die a slow, agonizing death.

Well, joke was on her.

"Mirror, mirror on the wall," I whispered to the mirror where I wiped away my makeup. "Who's the bitch gonna watch them fall?" My heart squeezed and I smiled, my dark brown eyes afire with vengeful hope. "That's right, cunt." Images of Hilary played through my head. "Your time is coming. You'll lose it all. Face humiliation. And be shredded in prison. No one likes pedophiles and I'll go to my grave making sure every single inmate knows exactly what you've done. Payback will be the most terrifying, agonizing, soul-crushing experience—you'll *wish* you could die."

Holt popped his head into the little dressing room at 7. "You good?"

The smile filling my face warmed me all over and I nodded. "Yep, I'll be ready in a bit."

"No hurry. I'm going to meet with Aiden and Felix about the New Year's Eve security, but we can leave whenever." He gave me a wink and closed the door behind him.

That man.

My heart clenched.

He had a terrible past, but he was so very, very good.

I just wished he could see it.

No one with a heart as black as he claimed his was could care for and protect someone the way Holt did me. We'd moved slowly in the sex department and he'd never once made me feel bad for needing things to be at my pace. Never once broke his patience. We hadn't had anal sex yet—and I truly believed Holt was completely on board if I said I never wanted that—but he made love to me each and every time he took me to bed.

Hell, that man made love to me with every gesture, every protective touch, every kiss, every moment he spent with me.

My hope for him was that he'd one day admit his heart was capable of love and deserving of being loved back.

And I'd be right there to give him that love.

It was hard to believe New Year's Eve was so close.

I'd been living at The Woods, involved with Holter, working at 7, and friends with the guys for several months. We'd absolutely flown through Thanksgiving.

Well, our version of Thanksgiving.

"Instead of celebrating Europeans repaying their Native allies by seizing Native land and imprisoning, enslaving, and executing Native people," Aiden explained the week before Thanksgiving, "we choose to raise money for organizations that support indigenous people—but we do that year-round, not just on one day. We celebrate what we're thankful for, but again, not just on one day. We continue to serve at the local food pantry and soup kitchen throughout the year."

Felix let Aiden pull him close and press a kiss to his temple before shrugging and saying, "We're always thankful, but we want to be thankful always and not just on a holiday that came about as a celebration of eradicating whole groups of people."

So, we'd had a special drag show at 7 on that Wednesday evening with all proceeds going to support indigenous people. It felt good knowing that every single show we produced raised money for so many well-deserving charities that supported oppressed and marginalized members of our community, our country, and our world.

The nine of us had also spent the whole day serving at the soup kitchen and, instead of shopping on Black Friday, we helped stock the local food pantry.

"Once Hilary is out of the way," I said, gesturing to the DeWitt name on both the soup kitchen and food pantry from our place on the sidewalk as we left after a long day, "I'm going to make sure both of these are doing the very best good they can be. I have a feeling Hilary keeps them going to look good, but is likely taking money from them that should be going to help others."

"You weren't kidding when you said your family name was all over this town," Holt said with a chuckle as he pulled me close.

"Nope. And my parents had every good intention. Hilary has nearly run everything into the ground, but not for much longer." Again, I had to be patient, but she'd be out of the picture soon enough, and I'd use my name to make sure the DeWitt name in Fairwood once again meant something *good*.

Once Thanksgiving had passed, Christmas came barreling through. We filled that holiday with small gifts for each other and more money raised for charities, buying gifts for as many children as possible, and helping several families have a holiday worth remembering.

The holiday season of my twenty-fifth year had been the best I could remember. Memories of my mother were few and far between—more like a warm feeling, fuzzy around the edges. What I remembered of my father was a mixed bag of what he used to be like before Mom passed, the severe grief after she passed, and the last few times I saw him when he was ill.

Every holiday since then had been full of sadness or horrors I never wanted to visit again, so celebrating by doing so much good while spending time with people I loved and trusted was a new experience in my life and I wanted to hold all the memories we made close to my heart and never let them go.

Knowing I had a home at The Woods for as long as I wanted it meant I could have all the good feelings and memory-making.

But would Holt stick around for any of it?

He'd seemed wary of the holidays and anything to do with *cheer*, but he'd stayed by my side through it all and I *knew* he'd had a good time. But friends, family, and happiness were as foreign to my dark-hearted man as gentle touches and trusting people were to me.

Maybe that was why we clicked and worked so well together. We both had so much trauma and pain in our pasts; so many years of having no one to make sure we were okay, no one to turn to.

I think it was why I so eagerly accepted the guys I'd come to think of as family and why Holt was so leery of it. He didn't *want* to like them and trust them—even though it was obvious that he *did*—and that was mostly because he wasn't sure *how* to be part of a family and friends.

He maybe didn't know how to do it, how to just let something feel good and accept it as it happened, but he was doing an amazing job of it.

Even when he fought it so hard.

But I hated the idea of him leaving when his lease was up.

The fact that he mentioned leaving almost daily—but maybe a bit less than when I first met him?—still worried me. Honestly, I wasn't sure he talked about leaving more as a way to prepare me for the eventual goodbye or to convince himself he still thought it was the right thing to do.

I hoped it was the latter and he'd finally realize he didn't *need* to leave.

Instead of wallowing in dread, I decided to enjoy the time we had together and work to build something between us he couldn't ever hope to leave.

"Hey, princess," Holt said as he cracked the door open. "We've got a problem. Can you come talk with me and the guys?"

My stomach dropped. "What is it?"

Holter held me close to his side as we made our way to the dining area of 7. The guys put me safely in the middle of the group and Holt drew his chair closer to mine, his big hand protectively gripping my knee. "Tell him," he said, his eyes flicking to Felix.

"Well," Felix paused to take a deep breath. "You know how Dodie is really good at recognizing faces?"

I nodded. It was one of the reasons Dodie was great at his security position at the bar.

"We made sure he knew what Hilary and her main guys looked like back when you first came to us," Felix explained, gesturing at Dodie for him to take over.

Dodie wrinkled his nose. "I'm pretty sure Hilary and her two goons have come to sniff around the last couple shows. First time, it was just a hunch. They couldn't get in because the show was sold out. Tonight, they still didn't get in, but I matched their faces with the images I'd seen when you first came here." He ran a hand through his hair. "She was pissy about not being able to get in. I could tell she *wanted* to drop her name to get by me, but she's at least somewhat smart enough to know we're likely on the lookout for her if she thinks you're with us." He shook his head. "Don't know if she was planning on using a fake ID or if she hadn't even thought it that far through. But she wanted in, probably to look around and see if anyone looked like her dead stepson."

I swallowed thick, burning bile. Hilary couldn't mess this up for me again. I didn't want to bring danger to my friends or our customers. And more than that—maybe it was selfish, but fuck it—I didn't want her anywhere near me. I wouldn't go back to what she did to me. I couldn't.

Gripping Holt's hand, trying to overcome the terror rather than drown in it, I blinked back tears. "We knew she'd probably start to get suspicious after a while. What are we going to do?" I asked around the lump in my throat. "I can't let her keep controlling my life, not after I've had a taste of being away from her—"

"Shhh." Holt squeezed my hand. "You'll never go back there. I'll drop her with a bullet right between the eyes before I let that happen." He pressed a possessive, protective kiss to the side of my face. "We've got a plan."

With a huge shaky breath, I nodded. "Okay. That's good. Because my brain just short-circuited. I want to be strong and fight, but the memories are paralyzing when I think about her."

The guys all nodded and their support gave me a strong boost of courage.

"So, we're going to let her come in—"

My eyes flew to Aiden as panic filled me.

"Let him explain," Holt murmured.

"We'll let her in for one of the New Year's Eve shows. She'll see this guy people call Snow and Mira-Mira, the drag queen no one can stop talking about," Aiden went on.

"And you'll be able to keep her from getting to me?" I asked, my words coming out in a rush. I wanted to trust them, but I knew how evil Hilary was.

"Yep," Dodie said, beaming.

I nodded. "Okay. I trust you. But *how*?"

Felix took my other hand. "You won't be here."

"What?" Now my head whipped the other direction to see if Felix was joking. "What do you mean? I *have* to be here. It's one of the biggest nights of the year." My wild eyes found Holt's determined gaze. "Holt? No. I just said I wasn't letting her control me anymore. Is that what my life will be now? Just constantly on the lookout and hiding?"

Holt cleared his throat. "I know you don't like it, but I think it's our best bet."

Hot tears welled in my eyes. "So, I sit at home, missing out on something I love, something I'm good at, just because that psychotic cunt can't accept that I don't belong to her anymore?" I stood as my voice got louder, knocking away Holt's hand when he reached for me.

Aiden was the one who finally got me to listen. He stood directly in front of me, hands on my shoulders, eyes boring into mine. "Zane, listen to me. More than anything, we want this bitch to go down in flames. If we ban her, it's going to look suspicious and probably bring more attention from her. If we let her in while you're here, she's going to *know* you're alive. So, we figure we can let her in, fake her out by having Snow and Mira-Mira being someone else, and then she goes on her merry way. It might not keep her away forever, but it should buy more time while the investigation gathers enough to bring her down."

His words sank in and, deep in my heart, I knew it was the best plan.

I didn't like it.

But it made sense.

While part of me wanted to just take her out the second she walked through the doors, I knew I'd regret it later if she was dead and not around to suffer when she was charged—and, god-willing, sentenced.

I dropped onto Holt's lap. "I understand," I whispered. "I just love it here so much. I don't want to be stuck at home while someone else does my show all because of that evil cunt."

"You won't be at home," Dodie said with a big smile. "Holt's going to take you away."

Holt groaned into my shoulder. "Well, there goes *that* surprise."

Dodie winced. "My bad. I just didn't want him to look so sad."

We wrapped up the discussion and I gave the guys hugs. "Have a great New Year. I'll see you once you say it's safe to come back." A strange, sad warmth surrounded my heart as I realized I had people to worry about me and let me know it was safe to return.

Later, when Holt held the door open for me, I hooked my arm in his as we walked into the icy air. "So, where are we going?"

Holt grunted. "Dodie has a big mouth."

"Yeah, but he did it for good reasons. Don't be mad at him. You were going to have to tell me sooner or later. Don't we have to leave?"

Holt nodded. "Yeah, need to head out tomorrow."

"To?"

He growled. "Can you let it be a surprise?"

"Are we driving or flying?"

"Flying." He must have realized I wasn't going to just let it go because he huffed and went on. "Thought we'd go shopping. I've got a guy who owns a place in a very private location in California. There are a lot of shops within driving distance, supposedly great restaurants, and we'll have a well-protected place to stay for however long until the guys say Hilary has given up."

My chest filled with goo. "Did you always want to take care of people?" I asked, our breaths puffing in tiny clouds as we made our way toward the car Holt had called for us. With Hilary suspecting I wasn't dead, it was best not to be out in the open walking around town.

Holt scoffed. "I don't take care of people."

I shook my head, clutching his arm tightly. "You do. Those bad guys you've brought in, hunted down, rid the world of? You did that to protect others. You don't do what you do just to make money and get off on it. You do what you do to protect people."

Holt was quiet as I climbed into the black car with tinted windows. He got in behind me and shut the door. "I've never really thought of it that way. I never set out to protect people, but I guess it's something I do without really even knowing why."

He didn't speak as the car made its way toward The Woods. Once we reached home, I rested my head against his shoulder while the car pulled to a stop. "I think you're drawn to protecting people because it heals the part of you that needed someone to take care of you. You didn't have that, so you give it to others."

Holt kept silent as we exited the car and made our way into the apartment.

He continued his silence as we readied ourselves for bed.

But when he wrapped his arms around me and pulled me close in the darkness of his bedroom, he finally spoke.

"I wish my younger self could have had someone protecting him. I wish *you* would have been safe from all of that nightmare." He pressed a kiss to my head. "But I'm grateful I'm able to help heal both of us by doing what I do now." Holt tipped my chin up, his mouth minty and warm as he captured my lips. "And just so you know, there's no way I was sending you away without me—I've never really taken a vacation, so you're stuck with me whether you like it or not."

I enjoyed the kiss that followed. The warm strength of his arms around me. "So, you want to spend New Year's with me?"

He smiled against my lips. "There is absolutely nowhere on this planet I'd rather be than next to you, princess."

Maybe there was a chance he'd stay after all.

Or maybe it was time for me to consider that perhaps my place was next to Holt, whether that was in Fairwood or wherever he needed to move to next.

CHAPTER 11
HOLTER

We'd flown to a private location in California and been picked up by an employee of a guy I knew very early that morning—it seemed even earlier due to the time change. Once we'd been given the key codes and instructed to enjoy our stay, I'd tucked Zane next to me in the lavish guest bedroom and we'd slept for a few hours.

I'd woken to his hot little mouth on me and we'd spent our first waking moments of our impromptu vacation getting each other off in sunny California while trying not to think of Hilary Grimstead.

Zane hadn't been as in awe of the home as I was—he'd grown up in luxury, I most definitely had not. But he exclaimed it was a gorgeous home and thanked me profusely for the trip and keeping him safe. While he perused the home's library and eyed the indoor pool area, I wondered what my life would have been like had I been born into money.

Would my mom still have found herself addicted to drugs and alcohol?

Still ended up with men who had aggressive tendencies and treated her like shit?

What would it have been like to live in a permanent home, with an actual bed in a real bedroom, and not had to move every three to six months?

"You okay?" Zane asked, pulling me from my thoughts.

"Yeah. You wanna swim?"

"Maybe later," he'd answered. "Can we go shopping? I'm excited about all the little shops we saw coming in."

So, we'd spent the day walking quiet paths between quaint little shops, stopping in nearly every single store, and sampling fun foods and wines. Zane bought a huge sun hat and sunglasses in our first store and proceeded to sashay his way from shop to shop looking like a god damn celebrity in disguise. His flowy, gauzy white blouse, tight, royal-blue pants, and slim black leather ankle boots were the perfect seaside, winter look with his hat and sunglasses and people in town ate it up. No doubt, they thought someone big was in their midst.

And they weren't wrong.

Zane DeWitt *was* something big. Big heart, big strength, big future ahead of him.

With you by his side if you'd just admit you want to stay.

"These wines are good, but I don't want to get tipsy," Zane said at lunch as we worked our way through a wine flight and our fresh seafood lunch at a table overlooking the sea. "If I drank all of these, I'd be beyond buzzed." He narrowed his eyes. "Why aren't you affected?"

I chuckled. "You might be about my height, but I outweigh you by at least seventy-five pounds. My tolerance is a lot higher."

"But you don't really drink that much."

Shrugging, I finished the wine. "It's just the way it works. It takes a lot more to get me drunk than it would you."

After lunch—Zane surprised me by turning down dessert, his sweet tooth usually took over—we shopped some more. Zane had inheritance money that he'd put aside and deemed it *only* for doing good in Fairwood. He made a decent amount bartending and dancing at 7. But he likely could have lived on tips alone.

For someone with a very comfortable amount of money, he was a bargain hunter and got super excited when he found a deal. On the flip side, he'd blow a stupid amount on makeup, costumes, and gifts for friends.

"The makeup and costumes will bring in money," he said with a shrug. "The gifts for friends just make me feel good."

When we'd visited each and every shop in town, we headed back toward our little home-away-from-home.

"Have the guys called?" Zane asked, his arm hooked in mine.

"No. They're probably busy. We can reach out tomorrow and see if the plan worked."

He pursed his lips but nodded. "I hate not being there, but this little trip has been fun so far." Curling into my side, he rested his head on my shoulder. "It's colder here than I thought it would be," he said.

"Well, it's winter." I kissed the top of his head, pulling him closer to warm him up.

"Yeah, but it's California."

"You're lucky it's southern California. If we were up north, you'd be shivering."

"Let's start a fire and cuddle up," Zane suggested.

"Sounds like a plan. You wanna stop at the little grocery and pick out some food for dinner and breakfast so we don't have to get back out?"

Zane nodded and stayed tucked against me until we reached the grocer.

As we perused the aisles and picked out some snacks, drinks, and food, Zane's eyes wandered. "You good?" I asked.

"Oh, um, yeah. I need to pee. And I think I forgot toothpaste."

"You can borrow mine."

"Okay," he said through a fake grin. "I'll just meet you up front. I think the bathrooms were that way."

"The bathrooms are in that back corner," I said, pointing to a big, conspicuous sign with the word RESTROOM on it. "You sure you're okay?"

He nodded. "Yeah, fine. I'll meet you at the front door."

If we'd been in Fairwood, I never would have let him out of my sight with Hilary snooping around. But we were nearly two thousand miles from home, so I watched Zane move toward the restroom. The nervous glance he threw over his shoulder had me scowling. "What are you up to, princess?" I muttered.

Deciding we'd have waffles, omelets, and bacon for

breakfast, I grabbed all the ingredients and made my way up front.

Where I found Zane standing by the door with a bag in hand and his bottom lip caught between his teeth. Narrowing my eyes, I glanced from the bag to his half-excited, half-guilty expression. Turning back to the cashier, I grunted and mumbled my way through unnecessary small-talk, paid for the groceries, and walked toward Zane.

"What'd you get? Could have just put it in with the rest of it."

He clutched the bag to his chest. "Just some—*stuff*—I wanted. No big deal."

Zane was a lot of things. Gorgeous, strong, courageous, and he had a heart of gold.

What he *wasn't* was a good liar.

But I just nodded and played along. He didn't *owe* me an explanation. If he wanted to purchase something secretly, that was his business. In fact, an arrow of warmth shot through me to realize Zane trusted me enough to know I wouldn't force him to tell me what he bought.

Instead of walking the rest of the way to the house, I ordered a car. While we waited, Zane proudly bought the biggest apple I'd ever seen from a little roadside fruit seller. He bit into the shiny fruit, juice exploding and running down his chin.

Laughing at him, I bent and kissed his lips even as he chewed. "You're gonna be a sticky mess."

Zane giggled and offered me the apple. Rolling my eyes at the things this man had me doing, I took a big bite of the crisp fruit. The fiery heat in Zane's eyes had me attempting to adjust my dick as he watched me chew.

We finished off the apple just as our ride pulled up. The drive was short and we were soon carrying our groceries and shopping bags into the house.

Once I'd set the alarm, I carried the groceries to the kitchen and began to unload everything.

"Wanna swim?" Zane asked once he'd returned to the kitchen from putting his bags down. "I don't know when the last time I went swimming was." He got a faraway look in his eyes. "Probably at school after Dad died and before Hilary made me come home."

I winced. "I'll watch you. I'm not a swimmer."

Zane's eyes shot to mine. "You don't like swimming?"

"Never done it."

His eyes grew wide. "I won't force you, but I'd love to get in the water with you for your first time. There's a shallow end. You could sit on the steps. I guarantee it's a heated pool."

That's how I ended up in the lavish pool, sitting on the steps in my boxers, while Zane swam laps. The warm water lapped at my shoulders as I watched his long, lean body glide through the crystal surface.

We made out for a bit on the steps, but called it quits before anything got too heavy since we weren't sure about cameras around the pool.

"How about we shower and then get that fire started. Are you hungry?"

Zane shook his head. "Not hungry yet."

"Fire and bed? I bet the view at night is spectacular.

I saw something today about a drone show taking place over the water tonight. Watch the ball drop later?"

Zane nodded, shivering as I wrapped him in a plush towel.

"Um, can I have the bathroom to myself for a while?" Zane asked, a blush staining his cheeks and all the way to his ears as he dripped water.

"Sure, princess. You never have to ask for privacy." I kissed his nose and then his forehead. "Wanna enjoy those double shower heads all by yourself?"

"Um, yeah," he answered and we headed into the main part of the house, locking the door to the pool behind us.

Zane took off toward the guest room and I heard the water turn on.

Making my way into our shared room, I smiled as I heard him singing behind the closed bathroom door. I grabbed a pair of sweats and headed toward the small hall bathroom.

After shampoo and soap, I dried and stepped into the sweats before tossing the towel down the laundry chute as we'd been instructed. Turning the lights down low, I got a fire going in the fireplace and turned on the television. The bedroom was laid out so you could see the ocean from the bed while still enjoying the fireplace and watching TV.

I stood by the window and watched the first few drones light up the night sky. When the bathroom door clicked open, I smiled and breathed deeply. The steamy scent of soap filled the air and I groaned appreciatively as

Zane's warm, damp arms wrapped around me, his sweet, hot mouth pressing kisses to my neck.

We stood like that for several moments, just enjoying each other's presence.

"Make love to me," he murmured against my shoulder.

And just like that, my world flipped upside down.

"Princess," I whispered, turning to wrap him in my arms, terror and longing warring through my body.

"Please, Holt. I'm ready. I've been thinking about it even before we came here. I bought stuff to prep—"

"You little shit," I growled, tickling his ribs. "Is that what you bought? I thought you splurged on lipstick or lash glue."

Zane giggled, dropping his head back so I could kiss his neck. "I'm ready. I want to leave the bad, ugly shit behind and bring in the new year with you."

"You've got me." I pressed my forehead to his and breathed him in. "I'm here, sex or no sex."

And he did.

Have me.

Body, heart, and soul.

And that was fucking terrifying.

I had no clue what to do with it, but there it was.

Zane owned me.

Zane pulled back. "I believe you." He caressed the side of my face. "I truly do believe that this thing between us could go on and on without changing the sex." He dipped his chin, leaning his head against my shoulder. "And if you don't want to go any further, I can respect that."

"It's not that I don't want to." I tipped his chin up, making him look at me. "Mainly, I'm scared of taking you back to the bad times. But I also don't want you to think that whatever this is between us is any less just because we're not having a certain type of sex. I'm one hundred percent satisfied with what we're doing—it doesn't change the way I feel about you in any way."

Zane smiled. "First, I get what you're saying. I'm kinda scared too." He brushed his lips over mine. "But we do a good job talking things through; I know you'd never hurt me and you'll stop if anything triggers the bad shit."

I nodded, drawing in a deep breath, loving the warm softness of his body against mine.

He went on. "And I know the type of sex we're having doesn't change the way you feel..." His bottom lip caught between his teeth. "I know it because..." He paused, his eyes welling up.

"Hey, what's wrong?"

Zane shook his head. "It's not bad, just a lot. Everything went to shit when my mom died. Then it got worse. Then the worse turned even worse and the damn nightmare started. I used to dream of falling in love, finding someone who would love me and treat me good; someone who would *never* hurt me and who would love me for *me* and not just for my body."

I tucked him close, cupping the back of his head in my palm and just soaking up his pain.

Zane took a shuddering breath. "And then I met you," his big brown eyes met mine and he pressed a kiss to my chin, "and my dreams came true." Before I could speak, he went on. "I don't expect you to say anything, but I need you to know, Holt. I'm in love with you. I *love* you. You are every good thing I ever dreamed of having in my life." He took my hand in his and brought it to his lips. "I love you," he whispered with so much feeling my heart nearly exploded. "And I want more than anything for you to make love to me."

I nodded, pressing a kiss to the spot right between his eyes. "You own me," I answered, my gruff words coming from deep within my heart. "I would do *anything* for you." Cupping his face, I kissed his fluttering lashes, his cheeks, his nose, and hovered over his lips. "You're the twist I never saw coming. I pride myself on being aware and observant, but you came into my life and blew me to smithereens." Words I'd never said to another human being hung heavy on my tongue. Letting out a long, slow breath—knowing nothing and everything hinged on these words—I whispered, "I love you." And just like that, the metal cage around my heart loosened and I saw wisps of a future with Zane. "I love you," I repeated like a prayer. "And I'll stand by you for as long as you'll have me."

His hot tears soaked my thumbs and I bent to press warm, wet kisses to his lips as our tears mingled. When he rocked his hips into me, our cocks brushing together, Zane groaned. His open mouth invited me in and my tongue stroked his as he pressed hands to my chest and pushed me toward the bed.

Chuckling as I bounced onto the mattress, I shimmied out of the sweats and moved myself to the middle, my eyes never leaving Zane. "It's your show, princess."

He nodded, his plump bottom lip caught between his teeth. Stripping the gigantic t-shirt he wore over his head, he moved quickly to his overnight bag. Producing a bottle of lube, Zane watched me as he placed it on the bedside table and climbed his beautiful, naked body onto the mattress.

Loving the way he took control—not because I wanted to be controlled, but because he trusted me enough to explore without worrying—I groaned when Zane straddled my chest and bent at the waist to press hot, open-mouthed kisses to my cock. The position put his hard cock pressing against my chest, his balls at my chin, and his tight hole at the perfect mouth-level.

Knowing exactly what he wanted from me, I gripped his cheeks and pressed a kiss to his pucker. Zane whimpered, spreading his legs for better access, and swirled his tongue around my dick. No words were needed as he sucked me and I worked him open. Savoring the feel of his ass in my hands, I pressed my tongue into his hole over and over, loving the way he rutted his cock against my chest and pushed his ass back to my face.

When he popped off my dick, the hard, slick flesh slapping against my belly, I blew a gentle breath against his pucker and smiled when he shivered. Zane moved from my chest, grabbed the lube, and repositioned himself over my waist. "This way first, just to get used to it. Then I want you on top of me." He pumped the slick liquid onto his fingers, reached behind himself to smear it over his hole, and then grabbed my cock.

Once we were both slick, Zane guided the thick head

of my cock to his entrance and closed his eyes. But he opened them quickly and glued his gaze to my face as he lowered himself inch-by-inch down my shaft. Leaning forward slightly, he pressed his hands against my chest and whimpered as his body stretched around me.

With my hands rubbing gentle circles on his thighs, I let Zane set the pace and refused to thrust my hips until I knew he was ready. "You good?" I asked, my words rough with worry.

He nodded. "Yeah," he panted, his fingers digging into my chest. "Just really full." His hand cupped my cheek. "Gotta stay present," he whispered and I knew his eyes on mine, clutching my chest, and touching my face were all ways he was keeping himself in the moment and not allowing the past in.

Zane began to rock his hips and the tight heat engulfing my cock nearly incinerated me. Gripping his hips, I let him go hard and fast before he slowed his hips to a sensual rolling.

Just as the grip of his body on my cock was about to be too much and send me over the edge, Zane shifted. Both of us groaned when my cock slipped from his body, but he scrambled to his back. Moving a pillow under this ass, I took my place between his spread legs and nudged my leaking cock to his hole. As much as I wanted to slide into his heat, I knew Zane needed to be the one leading this show in order to keep the demons at bay.

"Holt," Zane choked out. "Holt, please." He reached for my hip, encouraging me forward. "I need you inside me."

Pressing into him, I moved slowly, letting his body

adjust as he opened for me. Zane's eyes bore into mine, little whimpers and puffs of air escaping his lips with each inch of gentle invasion.

I'd never made love to anyone before. I fucked and left.

But Zane deserved so much more. He deserved soft and gentle, loving touches, sweet kisses, and orgasms that touched his soul.

As if you could touch this man in any way that wasn't *making love to him.*

When my balls pressed against his warm skin, I paused, my eyes caught on his hooded gaze, waiting. "Are you okay?"

He nodded, his eyes shimmering with tears. "I don't think I can come this way, but I want to feel you moving inside me. Wanna feel your cum."

Leaning over him, his legs spreading wider and wrapping around my waist, I brought our chests together. Anchoring my arms under his shoulders, I held him close as I pumped into him over and over. Zane's hand cupped the back of my neck and brought my face close to his, his lips capturing mine on a cry of pleasure. Our tongues danced, their rhythm matching the slide of my cock in and out of his tight heat.

Pulling away to shift his hips up slightly, I changed the angle of my thrusts just enough to peg his prostate. Zane cried out over and over as I stroked the sensitive bundle of nerves deep inside.

"Please, Holt," he gasped. "Give it to me. Come in me, wanna feel it."

His pleading sent me over the edge and I stilled my

hips, my cock pulsing deep, filling him with my load as I grunted and groaned through my orgasm. Staying inside until the last of my cum spilled into him, I finally pulled out slowly and shifted to his side. Stroking his soft cock, I trailed kisses over his nipples and down his torso.

I stopped at his quickly hardening dick and caught his eyes. "Can I suck you off and finger your ass?"

Zane let loose a sob, his cock twitching in my hand. "Fuck, yes."

Propping myself up on one elbow, I let go of his cock and trailed my fingers down to cup his balls and tease his taint. Working a finger between his cheeks, I pressed at his well-fucked hole. "Fuck, princess, I can feel my cum. You're slick with it, it's leaking from your ass."

He whimpered, his pucker clenching around my digit as I started to finger fuck him, pushing my cum back into him over and over.

"Suck me," he demanded. "Make me come."

Bending slightly, I took his cock in my mouth and swirled my tongue around his leaking head. He hadn't been hard earlier, but his shaft throbbed in my mouth now and I knew it meant a lot to him to be hard and near orgasm without any drugs forcing him toward the edge of a cliff he didn't want to jump from.

"Holt, please," he begged, his fingers tangled in my hair as he rode my fingers and thrust his cock between my greedy lips. "Oh god, please. I'm so close."

I curled my fingers deep inside, brushing over his prostate, and smiling when Zane bucked into my throat with a cry. His release coated my tongue, hot and thick, and I swallowed down everything he gave me as his ass clenched around my fingers.

Cuddling after sex wasn't something I'd done a lot of, but knowing Zane needed a comforting presence after he got off, I'd quickly learned to wrap him in my arms and hold him while we both came down from our orgasms. "You good?" I asked, my words gruff.

He nodded into me.

But a sniffle stopped me short.

"Hey," I whispered, pulling back to see his face. "Hey, what's wrong. Zane? Look at me."

He shook his head, teary eyes lifting to meet mine. "I'm good. Sorry. Nothing is wrong." Tears spilled down his face and gentle sobs shuddered through him.

"Shhhh," I whispered. "You're okay. I've got you."

When he finally calmed enough to speak, he swiped at his tears. "Sorry, I wasn't prepared for that."

"Wanna tell me about it?"

"It was just..." He paused, taking a shaky breath. "It was so good. It's always been so good with you, but *that* was a bone deep good I didn't even know existed. I always dreamed it could be like that, but never wanted to hope. Everything we do together helps erase the past —not that it's *gone*, but you help me block out the worst of it. Tonight helped to rewrite my story. Those chapters and scenes still happened, but my book has a chance to end differently now, because of you. You've given me new chapters to write."

Now tears streamed down my face and I pressed my forehead to his. "You have a beautiful, perfect story to write all by yourself," I whispered, my lips brushing over his. "But there's nowhere I'd rather be than by your side as you write it."

My entire life—from my birth, to the first time I killed a man, to my mother kicking me out—I'd never meant anything to anyone. My mom tried her best—at least, I'd like to think she did. But no one had ever wanted me by their side. True, maybe I'd never given anyone a chance, but it was different with Zane.

We loved and accepted each other, traumatic pasts, flaws, and all.

There was no question in my mind that I'd take this journey with Zane. In Fairwood or elsewhere remained to be seen, but I no longer wondered if we'd be better off apart.

Turned out, when I decided to fall in love with someone, I did it up right.

CHAPTER 12
ZANE

Holt made love to me again as fireworks lit up the sky and drones danced in delightful displays. He kissed me as the clock struck midnight and whispered his love for me as we drifted off to sleep.

When we woke, a new day, a new year dawning brightly outside as the sun sparkled on the sea, I took a deep, cleansing breath.

For the first time in my life, I wasn't just dreaming of things working out okay, I was certain they were going to. I could do it all without Holt, but having him by my side made it all the sweeter.

I pressed my ass back against his morning erection and groaned.

"You're not too sore?" he asked, his sleep-roughened words hot against the back of my neck.

"Just go slow and don't pin me down," I answered, knowing he'd understand and do everything in his power to make sex a positive experience for me. For someone with a questionable moral code and a shady past, he had to be the most loving, caring, absolute sweetheart of a man to ever walk the earth.

Holt pressed kisses to my shoulder and neck, one hand caressing down my chest and abs before stroking my cock. My ass clenched and I whimpered. "Do we need more lube?" he asked.

I wiggled my ass. "Check and see," I teased. Having fun and enjoying sex was such a new experience for me and I loved Holt for giving me the chance.

He grunted and shifted my top leg to the mattress as a finger trailed over my taint and teased my entrance. He slid in easily and groaned. "Do you know how fucking sexy it is to know you're slick with my cum like this? Fuck, princess." He pressed a kiss to my shoulder.

Even with prep and two prior rounds of sex, the stretch of his cock filling me took my breath away. Keeping himself on the mattress so as not to pin me down, Holter pumped in and out of me slowly, one hand tracing my arm until he gripped my hand and threaded our fingers together.

"I love you," he whispered.

On a half sob, half whimper, I choked out, "Love you, too," as he made love to me, my dick leaking all over the bed as I rutted into the sheets looking for release.

He fucked me slowly, gently, and thoroughly until my balls drew up tight. "Jerk yourself off." His demand had my cock twitching and I took myself in hand, stroking to the same slow rhythm of his thrusting hips.

I came with a silent cry, spilling over my hand, and clenching around his thick shaft. Holt grunted and stilled, his cock throbbing inside me as his hot release coated my insides.

He held me until the emotions subsided.

Moaning and stretching, I winced as his load leaked from my ass. "Oh my god, we need to shower and change these sheets. We've made an absolute mess."

So, we showered, switched the bedding, made our way to the laundry in the basement to wash a load of sheets, and fixed breakfast.

Wrapped in a blanket on the balcony overlooking the sea, Holt and I gobbled down bacon and homemade waffles. "We should probably check in with the guys and see how the plan with Hilary worked."

And we did.

A couple hours later after we made out and took a nap.

"Zane is here," Holt said as he put the guys on speaker phone. "What's the story?"

"She was definitely there looking for Zane," Dodie said. "We let her in without any fanfare. Figured it would look more suspicious if we made any kind of thing from it."

"We had Jesse stand in for you," Felix said. "He's your height, slim like you, and we had him in a dark wig. He wore your bar outfit and Mira-Mira nametag. A lot of the customers were either new or they were regulars who caught on quickly that there was a reason Jesse was pretending to be you."

Aiden spoke up. "Hilary beelined it to the bar after asking for Mira-Mira. Shoulda seen the look of disdain she had on her face when Jesse handed over her drink—

the kid isn't nearly as good behind the bar as you, but he served his purpose just fine."

"Hilary bullied some folks out of front row seats," Dodie said. "We privately reimbursed them and thanked them for understanding. They're coming to another show for free."

"We wanted her front and center to see Mira-Mira and figure out it wasn't you," Felix said.

"She was *pissed* when Mira walked onto the stage," Dodie crowed.

"Well, I think quite a few people were pissed," Aiden said. "Jesse isn't a performer."

"Awww," I murmured. "I'll have to thank him. I'm sure he was hating every second of it."

"He wasn't *that* bad, he just wasn't you," Felix said. "But it worked. Hilary was overheard by me, Aiden, and Dodie saying that guy definitely isn't Zane and she wasn't sure what the hype was but Mira-Mira wasn't even that good. She took her cronies and stormed out as soon as Jesse left the stage."

"So, it worked?" I asked.

"Seems like it. For now," Aiden said.

"You think it's safe to come back?" Holter asked.

"Yeah," Dodie said. "She'd heard tell of Mira-Mira and had reason to check it out thinking it was her precious stepson back from the dead. She knows now it's not. We'll keep an eye out for her, but I don't think she's coming back any time soon."

"If you can be here in time, the stage is yours tonight, babe," Felix said.

I couldn't help the grin filling my face. I raised a brow at Holt. "Can we get there in time?"

He wrapped his arm around me and pressed a kiss to my temple. "We'll be there. Let the fans know Mira-Mira is back."

The guys laughed and whooped while Holt disconnected the call and kissed me.

"Come on, we've got a flight to book."

Mira-Mira took the stage that night to a standing ovation and no one cheered louder or smiled broader than Holt.

CHAPTER 13
HOLT

Valentine's Day at 7 was dark, brooding, and sensual.

The evening was promoted as Anti-Valentine's Day and we'd pulled in an amazing crowd. All the employees had switched to all black and red uniforms and costumes, the lighting was dark, and the décor was anything but sweet and loving.

A huge contrast to the sappy-sweet way my heart beat for Zane.

Mira-Mira had easily taken over 7 as the biggest star and she ruled the stage each and every time she walked through the curtain.

She had two shows that night.

I watched as she danced around the stage in her black and red costume as her usual dark and broody music blared.

"You watch him with eyes that say he's an ice-cold drink of water and you're a man dying of thirst." Asa, the man I'd long-since started to consider a friend, cocked his head as he watched me. "But also like he's the most terrifying nightmare—like he's your worst fear all wrapped up in a pretty package."

"He is."

"Which?"

"Both."

Asa laughed. "How can he be the very thing you need and the thing you're most afraid of?"

I caught his eye, glanced toward where Dodie waited bar in Zane's absence, and raised my brows.

Pink flooded Asa's cheeks. "Touché." He watched Dodie for several seconds before turning back to me, my eyes glued to every move Zane made on stage.

"Guess we've got our very own *he fell first, but he fell harder* trope in The Woods," Asa said, a grin dancing on his lips.

"Huh?"

"It's a thing, ask any reader."

"I didn't..." My words slowed as I watched Mira-Mira. Fuck. "Okay, yeah, I did."

Asa smiled. "Nothing wrong with it. He feels the same. Anyone looking at the two of you can tell you're both head-over-heels. Does that mean you're staying?"

My heart beat faster.

Stay.

I'd never stayed anywhere before.

Part of me felt like I *had* to make a break for it. Beg Zane to go with me, leave town, start over. Having a *home* was as foreign to me as falling in love.

I didn't deserve stability.

Guys like me didn't get to call a place a home and live happily ever after.

But I didn't want to take Zane from a place he loved —a place he was slowly remaking into his home. And, if I was honest, I kinda liked it in Fairwood.

True, that was probably because of Zane and the guys, but still.

Would I be able to get out of the nine-month lease?

Would the guys even want me to stay?

Maybe I could share with Zane—

As if reading my mind, Asa smiled and bumped his shoulder against me. "You know that nine-month lease is completely ambiguous, right?"

"Huh?"

"You were so dead-set on not staying, needing a short-length lease." Asa shrugged. "I just said nine months to get you to sign. It's not really a binding lease —at least not in this situation."

I stared at him. "What?"

"You could leave tomorrow," he hedged. "Or you could stay indefinitely. For as long as you need it and want it, you've got a home with us. Zane, too. You're both family. We want you at The Woods if you'll have us."

This whole family, friends, love, and belonging thing was throwing me for a loop.

But I couldn't say I hated it.

Not even a little.

~

She buffed her blood-red nails as she studied herself with a wicked smile.

"Mirror, mirror, on the wall
Who's the fairest of them all?"

The mirror blinked out and showed a picture of raven-haired beauty dancing on a stage she recognized immediately.

"Zane DeWitt?" she gritted out. "That can't be.
His cold, dead heart was delivered to me.
Unless, of course, it was all a lie.
And now, my Zaney, he must die."

A blood-red fingernail trailed over a shiny green apple dripping with juice.

Placing the fruit in a gorgeous basket with five other apples, she wrote, "Zane, break a leg" on the notecard and tucked it into the basket.

"You're a tough little bastard to get rid of," she muttered. "But I *will* see you dead. You will *never* rule this town. *I* am the queen."

"Hey, who got the pretty fruit basket?" Dodie asked as he delivered it to the dressing room as I stood guard before the second round of performances. The crowd that night was huge and I didn't want Zane out of my sight. Hilary hadn't shown her face since New Year's, but we didn't want to take any chances.

All the queens clamored around in various states of dress and makeup as they prepared for the show. They ohh'd and ahh'd.

"Is there a card?"

"Who's it for?"

"Who sends *fruit*?"

"Bitch, we *are* fruity."

Cackles of laughter.

Dodie searched in the basket. "Ohhhh, it's for Zane."

Zane's pretty eyes flashed in the mirror as he stood to inspect the basket. "Oh my god, so pretty." He pouted and glanced at the other girls. "I'd share, but apples are my all-time favorite. I'm hogging them all." He carried the fruit to his makeup station. "But I'm not eating until *after* the show." Blowing a kiss my way, he winked. "I can't ruin a lip this fine."

"Whatever, bitch, no one wants your apples," one of the girls said. "Now, if that basket had been full of chocolate? The talons would have come out."

The room fell back into the cacophony of preparing for the show.

Every single girl had accepted Zane easily.

On one hand, it was likely because Zane and Mira were so kind-hearted and easy to like. On the other hand, most of the girls quickly realized that Mira's show was heart-stoppingly good. She brought in a ton of customers who in turn tipped the other girls well.

The other girls disappeared one-by-one to take the stage.

Then it was just me and Zane.

"Knock 'em dead," I said, my lips brushing his ear so as not to mess up Mira's makeup.

"Obviously," Mira purred. "Do you want to hang out here after the show or head home?"

"I'm down for either." I spread a hand over her cinched waist. "What do you feel like?"

Big brown eyes blinked up at me, fringed in smoky black and inch-long lashes. "Honestly?"

"Always."

"I want to untuck, wash my face, and spend the rest of the night cuddling. It's supposed to get nasty cold overnight and I want to be toasty warm at home."

"That sounds perfect. I'll be out front; come find me once you're ready."

Zane blew me a kiss as Mira-Mira sashayed toward the door to the stage.

~

Mira-Mira owned the stage as usual. The regulars knew Zane and I were a thing, but that didn't stop the whole crowd from drooling all over themselves as she finished her show and strutted her pretty ass off the stage.

Thirty minutes later, I'd seen most of the girls leave the dressing room. Mira had been the last to perform so it made sense she'd be the last to finish undressing

—I'd learned quickly there was *a lot* that went into drag.

"Hey," I asked Jesse as he came from delivering a round of drinks to the dressing room, "Zane look like he's almost done?"

Jesse grinned. "He was in his sweats, had his wig off. Most of his makeup was off, but he grabbed an apple as I was leaving. Looked like he was about to get pretty cozy with it."

I laughed. "That's Zane and his damn apples." Shaking my head, I figured I'd give him some privacy with his fruit before I dragged his ass home and tucked him into my bed.

Twenty minutes later, Dodie came rushing through the crowd with Aiden and Felix right behind him.

The look on their faces terrified me and I immediately stood, nearly knocking over the stool. It couldn't be Zane, I hadn't taken my eyes off the dressing room doors and those were the only two ways in and out of the space.

"What?" I demanded.

"Where's Zane?" Aiden asked.

"Getting undressed. I'm taking him home once he's done." I scowled. "Why?"

"Felix was playing through the security footage because one of the girls claimed she saw her ex in the crowd," Dodie explained. "I know the douchebag, so I was helping scan the faces."

"Okay?"

"Well, there was this old lady in line. She looked hella out of place, but she kept her face away from the cameras almost the whole time. Right when it was about her turn to get in, she whispered something to a guy in front of her and handed him a bag."

"Okay. Can we get to the fucking point?" I growled, my teeth grinding together.

"Just as she turned to leave the line, the camera picked up her face. She was disguised, but I swear it was Hilary."

My stomach sank.

"What was in the bag?" I demanded.

"Don't know. Couldn't find the guy she handed it to."

It didn't take a genius to figure it out, but I was clearly a dumbass.

"The fuckin' apples," I muttered and shot toward the dressing room. "Zane?" I bellowed as I burst through the door.

I didn't see him and there was no answer.

Fuck.

"Zane!"

As I rounded a corner, I saw him.

Shirtless, grey sweats, his black hair a mess, crumpled on the floor with a half-eaten apple next to him.

"Fuuuuck," I roared. "No, no, no. Call 911," I shot over my shoulder to whoever had followed me as I dropped to the ground next to Zane.

A very still, very lifeless, very colorless Zane.

The ambulance ride was an absolute blur.

The paramedics weren't happy to have me climb in the back, but they let me stay for the emergency drive to the hospital.

"What did he take?" one of the paramedics, Todd, asked.

"Don't know. A basket of apples was delivered to him by an old woman. He was eating one when he collapsed. We think something was in the apple."

"Like the wicked witch poisoned an apple?" the other guy, Brian, asked with disbelief etched over his face.

"Just like that," I mumbled. "And I'm gonna kill the cunt."

"Okay, moving on," Todd snapped. "We did *not* hear that. Grab the Narcan."

They worked in perfect sync placing oxygen over Zane's face, assessing his vitals. Monitors and an IV of fluids. A second dose of Narcan brought Zane around but he was still really out of it. I was frozen with fear, unable to comprehend anything through the panic over Zane and the determined chanting of *kill her, kill her, kill her* pounding through my veins.

The ER was worse because I was forced to sit in a damn waiting room while they worked on him. Aiden and Felix arrived and Aiden demanded an update as his employer. The nurse explained they'd assessed his airway and he didn't need to be intubated at this point. They'd started a second IV to draw several vials of blood and flush more fluid through him.

"Since the Narcan seemed to work, we can assume he ingested fentanyl or something similar, but we also want to get rid of anything else he might have taken," the nurse explained to an agitated Aiden as I paced behind him going out of my mind.

"He didn't take something," Felix said, the calmer of the three of us. "I've called the police to report someone drugging him."

The nurse looked skeptical, but she nodded and headed back to where they worked on Zane.

Aiden gripped my arm. "He's alive. That's what we have to focus on right now. He's breathing on his own, the Narcan worked, and they're taking precautions."

"I need to be with him." I felt the words all the way to my soul. Not being by Zane's side was a physical pain in my chest.

"They're not going to let anyone be in there just yet," Aiden said. "I've got his employee file where he listed you as his emergency contact."

My head whipped around. "He did?"

Aiden nodded and Felix winked. "Sure did. You then Asa. Damn good thing I review these often and make sure certain employees have the right people listed."

He squawked when I yanked him into a hug.

Felix came into the embrace smiling. "He's going to be okay."

"I'm gonna kill her," I growled.

"Let's focus on getting Zane out of here and healthy first," Felix said.

Two hours later, all seven of the guys sat in the waiting room with me. When a nurse came into the room, eight men held their breath. "Which one of you is his boss?"

Aiden stood up and moved closer. "I'm his employer.

I have his personnel file here that lists his emergency contacts." He handed over his ID and his phone with Zane's file.

I truly had no idea if Zane had really put me down as an emergency contact or if Aiden had done it, but I was grateful nonetheless.

"Mr.?" She glanced at the phone again. "Todd? Holter Todd?"

I stood. "That's me." Pulling my ID from my wallet—making sure to grab it rather than one of several fake ones I had shoved in there for when the need arose—I handed it to her.

"We'll let Mr. Todd see the patient. He won't be up for visitors until at least tomorrow, so it's best if you all go home to get some rest." The nurse gave us all a reassuring smile. "He's in good hands."

Aiden slapped me on the back and the rest of the guys mumbled their goodbyes as I followed the nurse through the swinging doors.

Zane was hooked up to an IV and a monitor. The steady beep-beep was somewhat comforting, but Zane's pale body looked so small and so fragile in the hospital bed.

"He's strong and he got the Narcan quickly. We think there was something else in his blood, but we'll have to wait to see what the lab results say. For now, we want to keep pushing the fluids and monitor him for a bit. The doctor will have the final say, but I'd bet he's going home by late afternoon tomorrow." She checked the clock. "Well, late afternoon today," she said with a kind smile. "I've done all the checks I need to do for now, so I'll let you both rest. There are blankets in the cabinet and you can use his restroom if needed." She positioned the call-button near the edge of the bed. "Push this if he needs anything. He can have ice chips and water if he wakes up thirsty. He's probably going to be pretty groggy and have a headache when he comes around. You can pull that chair closer if you'd like; it's not the Hilton, but you can at least stretch out a bit."

She dimmed the lights and left a slight crack in the door as she left the room.

And then we were alone.

Wasting no time, I pulled the recliner close to Zane's bedside and plopped down. Taking his hand, I brought it to my lips. "Fuck, princess," I choked out. "Fuck." I drew in a shaky breath, bowing my head with the back of his hand pressed to my forehead. "*Fuck.*" Hot tears spilled from my eyes and I let them fall. "I was so fucking scared." My gruff words filled the small room.

We sat there for a long time. I found the rhythmic beeps of the monitors and the gentle rise and fall of Zane's chest comforting. When the tears finally dried up and sleepiness replaced the extreme fear, I walked to the cabinet and grabbed two blankets. Spreading one over Zane first, I removed my boots, and settled back into the recliner. I pushed out the footstool and stretched, covering myself with the blanket. I'd lined the chair up just right. Reaching for Zane's hand, I laced our fingers together.

Coming down from the adrenaline allowed me to sleep fairly well. I didn't wake until the nurse popped in to take vitals and check Zane over.

Leaving him just long enough to wash my face, rinse my mouth out, and take a piss, I returned as the nurse was typing his information into the chart. "I think he'll go home today. We just need to see him awake and with it enough to take liquids, walk a bit, and eat something. Once we can do that, he'll likely be out of here." She finished typing. "I'll be back in a bit with some crackers and Sprite. If he wakes and needs the restroom, you can help him or call for me. Just know he's likely to be pretty weak."

I looked at a sleeping Zane after she left and scowled. He hadn't even woke up and they wanted to send him home? Don't get me wrong, I *wanted* him at home, but damn, how was he ready to leave?

Sitting back down, I took his hand. "Hey, princess. You need to wake up a bit. They're bringing you crackers and Sprite. You need to piss and walk and show them you're okay to go home." I took in his pale skin, dark hair, red lips and sighed. "I love you so damn much," I whispered. "Did you put me down as your emergency contact or did Aiden fudge that? I thought I was going to have to get angry and demand they let me in to see my boyfriend." I paused with a chuckle. "Instead, they led me right on in. No questions. So, if you put me down, thanks for that. If it was Aiden, I owe him big."

Zane's eyes fluttered open. "Boyfriend, huh?"

Tears sprang to my eyes and I grinned. "That's what you got from everything I said?"

He shrugged a thin shoulder. "Not every day that the guy I love claims me as his boyfriend."

I pressed his knuckles to my mouth. "Well, we did

things all backward. Saved you before I even knew you. Loved you before I even dated you. But, yeah, *boyfriend* if that's okay with you."

"Thought you weren't the relationship type?" Zane's big brown eyes were slightly more open and the sparkle was returning.

I stood and pulled him into a hug. "Yeah well, that was before I met you, princess. You changed just about every single square inch of my life." Kissing his forehead, I smiled. "Seems I'm the boyfriend and long-term relationship type these days. At least when it comes to you."

Zane sighed. "I can absolutely deal with that."

CHAPTER 14
ZANE

It took me about a week to feel back to normal.

The police had taken the basket, the apples, the note, and the video footage to use in their investigation against Hilary. The lead guy said they were within days of taking her in and the stunt she pulled trying to poison me to death was the last little bit they needed to close in on her.

Two days before the police planned on raiding her house, Holt walked into The Woods looking haggard and wild. "Come with me. I need you to see something."

He loaded me onto his motorcycle and took off.

We arrived a short time later at my father's house.

"Holt? What's going on?" I had good memories of this place buried deep, but I wasn't ready to revisit the bad shit.

"We're not going in." He entwined our fingers and led me to the small pool house. "I had a guy put her in here. I want to kill her. God, Zane, I want to kill her so badly. But I wanted you to get to see her and say your piece. You can shoot the cunt between the eyes if you want. Maim and disfigure her. Or just spit on her and walk away." He paused and cupped my face in his hands. "You don't even have to go in and see her. It's up to you. But I wanted you to have the choice."

My heart broke to see him in such turmoil. I knew exactly the feelings racing through him. Wanting her dead and gone for good. Wanting her to suffer. Wanting her to spend the rest of her life rotting in prison.

What was the right move?

I nodded. "I want to see her."

Holt tipped my chin and kissed me.

She was chained in the pool house. The cunt cackled when I walked in, fighting against her chains. I didn't question how they got her there, didn't wonder where her goons were. Honestly, I didn't want to know. I didn't care.

I stood there, facing her, and imagined hurting her the way she'd hurt me.

Let my brain play through what it would be like to kill her slowly.

In the end, I spoke in almost a whisper, refusing to give her the energy it took to raise my voice. "You tried to get rid of me, but I'm not going anywhere. Your plan was shit. All you did was bring the love of my life to me, so thanks for that. You wanted me to suffer and die, instead I'm thriving. I'm loved and I'm happy. Thank you. *You* made that happen.

"I used to be consumed by thoughts of killing you. Making you hurt." I shook my head. "Now? I don't even care. My one wish is that you live the rest of your life disfigured, as ugly on the outside as you are on the inside, penniless, left to rot in prison with every single prisoner knowing exactly what you do to children."

I clicked my long nails, ones I'd put on as a pick-me-up since I still couldn't perform. "I won't need to hurt you or kill you, they'll make you suffer to infinity and back every damn day. And I'll bask knowing you're rotting in jail, getting what you deserve, while I'm happy, in love, and spending every single DeWitt penny on making this town what Dad would have wanted it to be. Without you in it."

Hilary lifted her cold, dead eyes, snot and tears dripping from her face, her tangled hair hanging in a curtain. "If you think, for one moment—"

Without even thinking about it, my arm swung out. My hand connected *hard* with Hilary's face and I dug my sharp nails into her face.

"Who's the fairest of all now, bitch?" I asked, a nearly hysterical burble of laughter bubbling from deep inside.

Holt stepped near and took me in his arms. "Damn, that's gonna leave a *nice*, ugly-ass scar."

I took a deep breath and studied my stepmother as she screamed and fought against her chains. There was more I could do, but my heart and soul were well on their way to a happy forever with Holt and I just didn't have enough fucks to give.

"I hope they tear you apart."

Turning my back on her and walking away, I paused at the door to wait for Holt.

I knew that big strong man with his black heart and

questionable past could kill her in a heartbeat and never even blink an eye.

And I wouldn't love him any less.

Or, he'd take a page from my book and leave her for the police and for court cases that would likely take years to work through.

I stepped through the crack in the door, my back to them both, and just listened.

There was a loud slap and a scream.

"You'll never hurt anyone the way you hurt him. He is everything good in this world and you are everything evil. I hope you rot in prison. I hope they cut you open from end to end and let the maggots eat you from the inside out. This is for Zane."

I covered my ears and walked away as Hilary's screams shattered the cold, icy air.

Holt met me at the motorcycle, handed me my helmet, revved the engine, and we rode away.

Toward our very own fairytale happily ever after.

EPILOGUE
HOLTER

One Year Later- Valentine's Day

Valentine's Day dawned cold and snowy.

A perfect reason to keep Zane tucked in bed with me until we absolutely *had* to leave for 7.

No way was I keeping Mira-Mira from her adoring fans. She'd be upset and the customers would revolt.

We spent the morning wrapped up in each other's arms.

"Is a third orgasm your Valentine's Day gift to me?" Zane gasped as I took him in my mouth again, sliding my fingers into his cum-soaked ass.

"Nah," I said a moment later when I popped off his cock. "But it can be your gift to me," I teased.

By the time we finished, I wasn't sure either of us would be able to walk into 7 that night, and I had no clue how Zane would become Mira-Mira and dance like her life depended on it.

My phone buzzed.

"Ohhh, is that your contact at the prison?" Zane asked, his big brown eyes wide with excitement.

Ever since he'd figured out my one burner phone was *only* for my guy inside the prison to contact me, he kept his ears open for any peep the phone made.

I grabbed the phone and read the text.

"Well?" Zane demanded.

"Yep."

He giggled and slapped his hands against my chest. "Oh my god, tell me!"

I grabbed him around the waist and tossed him onto the bed.

"Nooo," Zane shrieked. "We have to shower."

Yanking his leg, I pulled him to the edge of the bed and picked him up, kissing him deeply. "Then let's shower."

Over the next several minutes, I filled Zane in on the information my guy sent.

What we already knew was Hilary was in maximum-security holding. She was on a twenty-four-seven watch so she couldn't take her own life. She spent most of her days begging people to kill her. She had major scars from the scratches Zane left on her face getting infected and a knife attack when she first arrived in prison.

"She's been put in medical because someone attacked her," I explained. "My man says the group held her down and finished the job on her hands."

Hilary had been missing the fingers and thumb on her right hand when the police had arrived to take her in on nearly one hundred twenty charges. Some of the charges stuck, some were dropped, but several new ones were brought against her.

"Finished?" Zane asked.

"Cut off the fingers and thumb on her left hand."

"Guess we'll never know exactly what happened before the police took her in," Zane mused in the open, curious, understanding way he always did when Hilary's disfigurement was brought up.

I shrugged. "Someone must have really wanted her to pay and never be able to hurt anyone else."

"So, the attackers maimed her even more?"

I nodded. "Guards ignored the cameras and the footage has conveniently disappeared, but the attackers were heard to say something in regards to *now she can't hurt any kids even if she gets out.*"

"She'll never get out, right?" Zane's words were laced with worry.

"No way. There are too many witnesses, too many victims, too much evidence, and too many charges. She will die before they reach the end of everything brought against her."

"And everyone in my notebook?"

"Dead or serving the rest of their lives in prison. Ruined, decimated, and won't ever see the light of day."

I'd made sure the people who hurt Zane would either be brought up on so many charges they'd never get out of the prison system.

Or they'd conveniently met with a deadly accident.

Zane took a deep breath. "Sometimes I feel guilty for not having a single ounce of remorse for Hilary and the buyers." He walked into my arms and sighed as my hand stroked up and down his back. "But then I realize their punishments are because of their choices, their actions, and they have to pay the price for the pain they caused."

And pay they will, I thought to myself, dark images of what my connections could ensure would take place in those holding cells filling my head.

But to Zane I nodded and lifted his chin for a kiss.

"I love you and you deserve every bit of happiness this life can give you. You are strong and courageous, and I'm lucky to call you mine."

We kissed for several minutes until Zane squeaked when he caught sight of the clock. "Oh my god, we're gonna be late."

"You're the star of the show, they'll wait."

But we rushed to 7 and I kissed Zane goodbye as he ran to the dressing rooms to become Mira-Mira.

The night was spectacular.

Surrounded by friends I considered family, watching the love of my life bring down the house, and getting to keep people safe were all things I counted on my list of ways to have a good evening.

Later that night, I hooted and hollered as Mira-Mira did her final death drop and crawled seductively to the front of the stage. Flipping her long, black hair out of her face, her eyes caught mine and she gave a smile meant only for me as she batted those smoky, smoldering eyes.

We were definitely looking into a round four before the night was done.

As we left 7 a couple hours later, I wrapped my arm around Zane. "You did amazing tonight, as usual."

"Thanks. It was a good show. Some of the new girls are *really* good."

"None as good as you, but I might be biased."

"I think I want to switch up my songs and maybe throw in a new costume and dance moves," Zane mused as we walked. "But right now, I'm exhausted."

"Let's go home, princess."

Home.

Fairwood.

The Woods.

The guys and 7.

All of them were *home* now.

But my true home would always be Zane.

"You're my home," Zane murmured against my cheek. "Always."

I turned and caught his lips. "Same."

"I'm serious, Holt. I'd go anywhere with you as long as we stayed together."

I nodded and kissed his nose. "Agreed. But I think I like here. Maybe we just fill *this* home with all the love and stick around for a while?"

"Always dreamed of getting my own happily ever after."

"There ya go, princess. Happily ever after."

ALSO BY A.D. ELLIS

Wrapped Up In Love- *A Holiday Collection*- this box set gathers the three books listed below into one value-priced set. Own all three books for LESS or read all three in one box set on Kindle Unlimited! Grab it HERE.

Holly Hills Christmas- **Holly Hills Christmas** is a steamy, feel-good, M/M age-gap holiday romance.

Listen to Your Heart- **Listen to Your Heart** is a steamy, second chance, M/M romance with just enough holiday magic to make you believe. It shares the same world with **Follow Your Heart** by Declan Rhodes.

The Heart of St. Nick- ***The Heart of St. Nick*** *is a steamy, forced proximity, small-town M/M holiday romance with a slight age gap between a bowtie and suspender-wearing good guy and an emotionally-stunted man with a cold heart just waiting to be melted.*

Two Weeks in Paradise- an opposites-attract, forced proximity M/M romance between two widowers nearing fifty. This low-angst love story is perfect for fans of kinky steam mixed with sweet fluff.

Jett & Leighton: On Cravenwood Block- a steamy, opposites-attract, bisexual-awakening, roommates-to-lovers M/M romance featuring a sexy-as-sin tattoo artist and a fresh, flashy barista with a smile that lights up the room.

The Perfect Blend- A steamy, M/M age-gap, marriage of convenience, coffee shop romance

Perfect Timing is a steamy, M/M romance with an introverted, demisexual writer and a big, soft teddy bear of a nurse trying to navigate a love they've always dreamed of but most definitely weren't expecting.

Adore (Remington Place 1) is a steamy, age-gap, bi-awakening, dad's best friend M/M romance with a sassy smartass and a sexy silver fox. It's the first book in the Remington Place series and can be read as a stand-alone.

Crave (Remington Place 2) is a steamy, friends-to-lovers, fake relationship M/M romance with a virgin nursing student and a gruff, grumbly construction worker.

Desire (Remington Place 3) is a steamy, age-gap, hurt/comfort M/M romance featuring a heart-of-gold mechanic and a twink who's a lot stronger than he realizes. *Please note: This story has mention of sex trafficking and sexual abuse.*

Yearn (Remington Place 4) - a steamy, enemies-to-lovers, forced proximity M/M romance between two EMS workers who have hated each other for a decade.

Power Struggle is a steamy M/M, age-gap, forced proximity romance set in a small town. A twenty-year history, rival schools and jobs, and a hotel with only one bed make for a hot and heavy, sweet and sexy, HEA-guaranteed love story.

Take Me Home M/M age-gap, opposites-attract romance with plenty of steam and a scene that will make you appreciate camouflage and work boots

Let Love In M/M age-gap, forced proximity, dad's best friend, bisexual-awakening romance. Available on AUDIO!

Let Love Win M/M brother's best friend romance. Available on AUDIO!

Buried Secrets Romantic suspense stand-alone title. Available on AUDIO!

Silver in the City (3 books- meet the Silver crew you read about in Forged in the City) Available on AUDIO!

Forged in the City (3 books- a spin-off series from Silver in the City) Available on AUDIO

The BJ Boys Series (3 books, small town, big love) Available on AUDIO

Forever Better Together (friends to lovers) Available on AUDIO!

His Reluctant Cowboy (age gap, opposites attract, cowboy romance) Available on AUDIO!

What Blooms Beneath (LGBT Fantasy romance) Available on AUDIO!

Sawyer

(this was the first M/M I wrote and you may remember Sawyer and Luke being mentioned in Barrett & Ivan as well as in Ryker & Gavin)

The Something About Him series has been revamped with revised stories, updated blurbs, and spiffy new covers.

The series is available on ALL of your favorite book platforms!

Bryan & Jase

Brody & Nick

Barrett & Ivan

Braeton & Drew

Ryker & Gavin

Kade & Cameron

A.D.'s first stories (all male/female except Sawyer which is male/male) are in the Torey Hope and Torey Hope: The Later Years series. Find the 8 book box set HERE or you can find each individual title on Amazon.

For Nicky

Because of Beckett

Christmas in Torey Hope

Loving Josie

Decker

Sawyer

Zach

Kendrick

About the Author

A.D. Ellis is an Indiana girl, born and raised. She spends much of her time in central Indiana as an instructional coach/teacher in the inner city of Indianapolis, being a mom to two amazing teenagers, and wondering how she and her husband of over two decades haven't driven each other insane yet. A lot of her time is also devoted to phone call avoidance and her hatred of cooking.

She loves chocolate, wine, pizza, and naps along with reading and writing romance. These loves don't leave much time for housework, much to the chagrin of her husband. Who would pick cleaning the house over a nap or a good book? She uses any extra time to increase her fluency in sarcasm.

A.D. uses she/they pronouns.

Sign up at http://www.subscribepage.com/ADEllisNewsMMRomance for a FREE books!

Website http://adellisauthor.com/

Find me EVERYWHERE at https://www.adellisauthor.com/mylinks/

CONNECT WITH A.D. ELLIS

Follow my website http://www.adellisauthor.com or find me on Facebook

http://www.facebook.com/adellisauthor

If you want to get updates about releases, interviews, sales, giveaways, and more please sign up for my newsletter http://www.subscribepage.com/ADEllisNewsMMRomance

To make it easy, find me EVERYWHERE here- https://www.adellisauthor.com/mylinks/

Acknowledgments

It's always so hard to write this part because I'm worried I'll forget someone without meaning to.

Thanks to Jamie H and Jamie P for medical input on this one.

And to Samrat, my amazing PA, who hardly ever gets enough appreciation. He's such an asset to me AND he made this cover, so he deserves a huge shout-out!

Gage usually gets a mention, but his encouragement and support on this one gave me the confidence to write it. Planning this story and bouncing ideas around with my best friend was a ton of fun.

Readers- you are the reason I write. As long as you continue reading my stories, I'll continue writing them. Thank you for your support.

Bloggers- your support, reviews, and promotion are very much appreciated. Thank you!

My author buddies- I don't know that I could keep doing this without our brainstorm sessions, laughter, road trips, meals, wine, and friendship as my support.

Thank you to my alpha readers, betas, editors, proofreaders, and ARC readers! Your eyes and input are beyond important to me.

Brett and Gage- as usual, I doubt you even grasp how much your support, input, and friendship mean to me.

This author journey has brought many wonderful things into my life, and you both are two of the BEST! I'm blessed to call you friends.

My family and friends- thank you for your love and support, always.

www.ingramcontent.com/pod-product-compliance
Lightning Source LLC
Chambersburg PA
CBHW030831020726
47499CB00006B/2152